Shadowed Soul

Book Six of The Gifted Series

Ana Ban

FIVE POINT PUBLISHING

For Jasmine

Contents

For a full family tree, please visit
www.anabannovels.com/gifted-tree

Chapter 1

Perched on a rock outcrop overlooking Cobb Valley, I paused for a moment to take in my surroundings. Breathing in the warm, sticky air, I watched a kārearea—a New Zealand falcon—make a swirling dive through the treetops in search of a snack. The untamed wilderness and tangle of caves sculpted by the river system were stunning and gave my adventurous heart a reason to beat. Taking one more deep breath into my lungs, I charged on, driven by some unknown force. Exploring the world had become an obsession. It had become my life.

"Come on, Aden," I called out with a teasing smile over my shoulder.

My brother grumbled but upped his pace. Though he didn't fully understand my desire to traipse through jungles or explore hidden caverns, he always supported my wild whims. Supporting was more important than understanding, anyway.

Reaching another small apex, I gazed down at the scenery below. A perfectly round opening a couple hundred feet below beckoned me closer. I'd never been able to resist the siren's call of unexplored nature, and there was something about the strangely symmetrical clearing that had me in its grip.

Though Aden gained on me, I didn't wait. Taking off at a sprint, I raced down the hill, long, blonde hair flying behind. Even in this heat, I liked to have the curling waves loose. It might be vain, but I enjoyed the feel of the wind whipping and pulling at the lengthy tendrils. The sensation reminded me of my father. He'd never get mad at me when I'd do something out of hand. He would only tug playfully at a curl and give me a wink.

I missed him so much. Aden had been my guardian for many years, and I loved him as much as one person could love another. He'd become more than my brother; he'd stepped into the role of both parents, as well. He called out to me now, his voice lost to the wind. "Wait for me!"

When I reached the edge of the clearing, I paused, one hand resting against the trunk of a beech tree. Nature had always felt like home to me, not the city with its overabundance of concrete and steel. Here, without a soul in sight, was where I felt at ease. Aden was the only other person I could stand to be around for any length of time.

Placing one foot in front of the other, I reached the center of the meadow and gazed up, allowing the bright sun to wash over me. Though still morning, the sun had already risen high in the Kahurangi National Park. New Zealand had turned out to be the perfect place to explore the untouched wilds to my heart's desire. Aden and I had been backpacking for the last two days—slinging up hammocks at night to sleep and catching trout to cook over portable stoves—and we'd yet to run into another person.

Peace and serenity settled into my chest, and I let out a happy sigh. But it didn't last.

Though the day remained warm, chills crept down my arms. What felt like dark sludge seemed to slide over my skin as dread washed through me. Turning slowly, I studied the surroundings, looking for something out of place. A large animal, intent on lunch? An incoming storm?

No, this was something else. The sky darkened as huge, winged shadows skittered along the ground. Heart in my throat, I searched frantically, unable to determine their source.

"Aurelia!" Aden's desperate cry could barely be heard above the ringing in my ears. I spun to face my brother, opening my mouth to answer him or shout a warning or simply scream, but I never got the chance for any of it.

I'd been surrounded.

They appeared from thin air. Five men—tall, broad-shouldered, dark gazes filled with malevolence—had formed a loose circle around me. As they closed ranks, I turned one way and then another, desperate for an opening to make my escape. The pure evil pouring off the vile creatures nearly choked me as the realization of my fate finally sank in.

Aden, poor Aden, with his warrior's spirit and soft heart, fought his way toward me, refusing to give in to the utter hopelessness of the situation. Two of the abhorrent men intercepted him. Still, Aden struggled to get through. To rescue me. The remaining three closed ranks until I was well and truly trapped, murmuring in a language I didn't understand.

Terrified, I watched as one of the creatures slammed his palms against my brother's chest. A scream escaped my lips as Aden crumpled to the ground, his face racked with pain, the fight gone from his vacant eyes.

ADEN!" MY HOARSE CRY WOKE me, and I sat up with a start with a palm against my pounding heart. Squeezing my eyes closed against the tears dampening my cheeks, I willed my heart back to normal.

This was why I avoided sleep at all costs. Every time I closed my eyes, no matter for how long or how in need of rest I was, the same memory always dredged to the surface. Lying back, I rested my arm across my forehead and breathed deeply. It had been years since that terrible, fateful day. Now, Aden was gone, and I was....

The alarm next to my bed blasted, startling me back into a sitting position. With a groan, I turned and slammed my palm against the button. Resting my head against the pillow, I briefly contemplated staying exactly where I was.

What did I have to live for, anyway? My family was gone. I couldn't stay in one place long enough to make friends. I only had one purpose: staying alive to hunt the creatures that had taken everything from me. Hunt them so no one else ever had to feel the way I did.

Rubbing my palms against my eyes, I sighed and sat up again, swinging my legs out from the thick covers and resting my feet against the floor. My hand dropped to my stomach, fingers smoothing across the angry red welt that had been a stab wound just hours earlier.

My injuries were taking too long to heal. It was time to feed.

Though I dreaded this particular action, it was necessary to continue my existence. Dressing in my typical uniform—black leather pants, a comfortable t-shirt, and a matching black leather bomber—I strapped a large belt around my hips. While it looked stylish to the unseasoned observer, it was also chock full of concealed weapons.

My long blonde hair hung down my back in beachy-wave style, and I covered my baby blue eyes with a pair of dark glasses. The sun, while not a danger to me, had a tendency to prick at my eyes and skin. Whenever possible, I avoided being outside during the apex of the day, but the night—the night was my time.

There were still a few hours until sunset and a couple more until I started my shift at the local tavern. That left me plenty of time to find the bastard who'd stabbed me and offer retribution. But first, the issue of dinner. Before leaving my small one-bedroom cabin, I reset the protection spells. No one would be able to enter here while I worked.

Using my speed, I made it to the village in seconds, pausing behind a small building that served as cover until I could check my surroundings. Once certain I was alone, I stepped onto the street of a small village nestled against the Moldoveanu Peak in Romania. For a moment, I simply breathed, appreciating the fresh air, before making my way toward the few stores lining the main street.

Though my blonde locks and pale skin were a stark reminder of my outsider status, I'd found the people of the village to be both welcoming and accommodating. The men who came into the tavern quietly lusted after me, while the typically conservative women watched me with envy in their eyes.

The children...well, I avoided contact with children whenever possible. It wasn't safe for them to be near me.

Two men I recognized from the tavern, Vasile and Nicolae, were loading grain into a wagon at the feed store. They were both physically fit, a father and son team that ran one of the farms just outside the village. They would come into the tavern to eat after a hard day but never stayed to drink. The man's wife had passed away a few years ago, and the son had stayed to help the family business.

Lifting a hand in greeting, I spoke in the local dialect. "Bună ziua. Ce faci?"

"Foarte bine," the older man answered. "Ce faci?"

"Bine, multumesc," I returned, then added, "but I could use your help."

The men glanced at each other and nodded. The son jumped down from the trailer, and they approached me together. "What do you need?"

"There's an order around back for the tavern," I said. "Perhaps you could help me load it into the cart?"

Once they agreed, they followed me to the back of the store. Checking first to make sure we were alone, I looked directly into Vasile's eyes and murmured an incantation. Nicolae watched with an open jaw before I turned my attention to him.

Once they were both under my control, I carefully eased my lengthened incisors into Vasile's wrist. I always preferred to have two or three men to take blood from so that I didn't leave any of them feeling unnecessarily woozy. After taking what I needed from Vasile and Nicolae, I placed a few Lei in both their pockets. It eased my guilt and gave them a little extra help.

It was the least I could do after sucking their blood.

Leaving them leaning against the wall, I walked away and found a spot just down the street to make sure no harm came to the pair while under my spell. I knew when they snapped out of their daydream that they would have no memory of our interaction. Once they blinked several times and shrugged at each other, they went back around to the front to finish their loading.

Breathing out a sigh of relief, glad for the distasteful task to be done, I continued on my way.

The immediate surge of energy after feeding always made me slightly sick, knowing that it took another person's life blood to sate my appetite. There were times I was able to infiltrate a blood bank to survive, but my nomadic lifestyle made even that a difficult thing. Having specialized coolers to keep the blood healthy tended to be more luggage than I was willing to carry.

Shaking these thoughts away, I went back to the scene of my tussle just before dawn to scrounge for any clues as to where this shadowman could be hiding. We'd fought in the hills, well away from the village. I'd led him there in order to keep the villagers safe—as safe as they could be with me near, anyway.

Ever since my escape, the shadowmen had been attempting to recapture me, but I'd been taught well. Even though my teachers had been evil, I'd sopped up as much information as they'd been willing to offer—and much more they hadn't.

There was only one creature that still frightened me because my blood ran through his veins—just as his ran through mine. Blood was a powerful thing, and it gave each of us the ability to track the other. For me, that meant staying far away.

I knew that one day, I would have to face Maurice. I also knew, on that day, that I would kill him.

He would die, and I would give my life in the effort.

Though it was cowardly to run, I spent my time learning my abilities, honing them into the weapons they were. Maurice had taught me everything he knew; in the years since I made sure to learn everything he didn't.

If that meant taking out more of these monsters along the way, I'd do so happily.

The blackened ground around me writhed in pain. Even with the darkness in my soul, the earth still called to me, spoke of its wonders and its woes. I sank down, digging my hands through the injured soil, and began to chant.

Mother Earth, giver of life. Darkness has descended upon you, caused you strife. Send me sage to cleanse this air. Send me copper; send me selenium; send me iodine; spread their richness for your ground to share. Dispel this evil once and for all; in your name, heed my call. Small shoots of green sprang up around me, already pushing out the evil stench of battle. With a grim smile, I asked Mother Earth for a favor in turn. *Lead me to the one who did this.*

Knowledge rushed through me; a detailed map pushed into my mind.

Thank you, I sent out before standing and facing my target. Using my preternatural speed, I raced along the ground, adjusting slightly as needed in order to take the most direct route to the shadowman. Several miles into the mountain, the trail abruptly ended.

Pausing, I took a long look around, my every sense flaring out. He was here somewhere.

My eyes spotted a small, dark object on the ground a hundred paces from where I stood. Stalking over to it, I bent to retrieve a single black feather.

So, he was injured but well enough to shift form and take flight. Mother Earth could only lead me so far; the secrets of the wind were more difficult for me to unearth. For now, I could do nothing but return to the village. Though I preferred to keep this away from the innocent humans, I knew the shadowman would be back to finish what he started.

And I would be waiting.

Chapter 2

The tavern remained quiet all night. As I lazily wiped the counter, I watched the minutes crawling by. Given the scarcity of customers, I tended the establishment solo, save for the lone cook manning the kitchen. Serving as both barkeep and server was a role that suited me fine.

This type of work was easiest to get and easiest to leave. Though I preferred to be outdoors, this job gave me a good insight into people and allowed me to immerse myself in the local gossip and oddities quicker than anything else could have.

I could eavesdrop at will, turning up the volume whenever it suited me. Tonight, I felt bored and restless enough that I listened in on each conversation being held. Vlad, in the corner, complained about the quality of chicken feed in the last several orders. Denis spoke about his wife and how she wished to live in a bigger city.

It was all idle chit-chat that did nothing to spark or keep my interest.

As the evening turned to night, only a few of the regulars remained. Though I'd ditched the jacket while I worked, my body temperature stayed warm.

I was always warm. One of the benefits of the creature I'd become.

Which was why, when chills suddenly crept up my arms, I immediately snapped to attention. When a feeling of dread washed over me just moments later, it all clicked.

There was a shadowman nearby.

The door opened with a gust of early summer wind—the kind that hinted at warmth but still raised goosebumps along the flesh. A man stood in shadow, hesitating in the doorway to survey the room. My left hand dropped to my belt, preparing to grab a weapon as needed.

As the shadowman studied the room, I did a quick scan of the remaining stragglers, wishing I could get them to safety before this fight ensued. Instead, I would do my best to take the fight outside.

On my terms.

"Dorin," I called back to the cook with a steady voice. "Cover me."

The moment I uttered a word, the stranger's dark gaze instantly switched to mine, and I felt the look down to my toes. Their intense stare seemed to penetrate straight through me. An icy shudder ran down my spine, accompanied by an odd heatwave searing along my veins.

That was new.

As the shadowman stepped fully into the room, his face became visible in the dim light. He had a strong jaw and striking green eyes. His body had been built for fighting; his shoulders were broad, and his muscles lean.

I swallowed once, hard, before taking a step back. Another step placed me just outside the bar area and closer to the door. Keeping my gaze steady on the stranger, I continued to back up until I could feel the knob of the door at my back.

"We don't need to involve anyone here," I said so softly no one in the room would be able to hear. No one but the dark man who hadn't taken his eyes off me.

Though he paused in surprise, the man tracked my movements, his attention wholly on me. That was good; that was what I wanted. Never mind my racing heart and strange reaction to this evil creature. If his attention stayed on me, that meant he would follow me—out the door and away from the humans.

Dorin appeared at the bar, wiping his hands on the apron around his waist. He gave me a wink to let me know he had it handled, and when my eyes flicked back to the shadowman, I registered an oddly jealous look on his face.

"Be right back," I murmured in Romanian, just loud enough for Dorin to hear. My right hand reached back to turn the knob, and I stumbled into the alley, deserted at this time of night. I'd lost eye contact with the frightening man but backed several feet away, keeping my focus on the door.

A huge, winged shadow fell across my form, and I automatically looked up to track its movements. The tricky thing about shadowmen was even when they were invisible to the naked eye, their evil stench still left a telltale shadow. I'd come to realize only the shadowmen and I could see the shadows. Perhaps the rest of humanity was just ignorant enough of the evils of the world to be blissful.

There wasn't a sound, but I sensed a presence behind me. With a movement quicker than a speeding bullet, I detached a knife from my belt, spun, and let it fly with deadly accuracy.

The shadowman tossed it aside with a flick of his wrist, amusement plastered on his face. This was not the man from inside the tavern but the same shadowman I'd been tracking in the mountains. The one who had stabbed me just twelve hours earlier.

"Enough of these games. You will come with me now."

"In your dreams, dickhead," I shot back, using insult as a way to anchor myself.

Without another word, I lunged toward the creature, two more knives in my fists. Though I could easily shift into an animal form, I always felt more confident in my natural state.

Our bodies crashed into each other with an impact that resounded more thunderously than a semi-truck smashing through a concrete barrier. I cringed internally, praying the patrons within the pub had the good sense to remain indoors.

As we exchanged blows, I managed to swipe across his belly with my knife and, almost more satisfying, directly across his cheek. I allowed a small smirk; with a snarl, the shadowman backhanded me, hitting high on my right side. I went spinning, angry with myself for getting cocky. Landing with an oomph several feet away, I paused just a moment to collect my rattling brain.

I barely had time to turn onto my back before the shadowman dragged me up by my shoulders, tightening his grip painfully and sneering into my face. Drool spewed from his once-handsome face. "You will learn respect, woman. You're mine now."

"Don't you wish," I said with a smile, blood trailing down my cheek. In my tumble, I'd managed to keep hold of one knife, and I gripped it tightly in my right hand. I surged forward with the sharp blade, but before I made contact, two things happened simultaneously.

The shadowman's face crumpled in pain, and another dark form inserted itself between the shadowman and me.

With the knife already on a forward trajectory, I couldn't have stopped even if I wanted to. The blade sank deep, and I stepped back with a gasp, unable to fully comprehend what had just happened.

The shadowman I'd been fighting dropped to the ground, agony stamped on every feature. His hands covered his ears as he let out an otherworldly, blood-curdling shriek. Dark blood soaked the ground, dripping from his ears, eyes, and mouth. I watched, horrified, unable to move or look away from the gruesome sight.

As he gurgled out his last breath, the stranger who had arrived just moments too soon turned to fully face me.

The man from the tavern.

A shadowman. Evil, like the man that now lay dead at our feet. No matter the glittering green eyes that seemed to pierce into my very soul or the skittering heat that danced through my veins when I snagged on his gaze. This man was evil and needed to die alongside his friend on the ground.

"Are you all right?" the creature asked, his eyes raking down my body and back up again. There was nothing sexual in the perusal; it was as if he were actually concerned for my wellbeing. It didn't stop my stomach from clenching in a purely feminine reaction.

Before I could move or respond, the man collapsed to his knees. His right hand reached back and retrieved the knife still lodged in his kidney. It clattered to the ground, and we both stared at it for a beat of time.

"Get to safety," he murmured before collapsing.

My jaw hung open, unable to believe my ears or piece together what had just happened. *Finish him*, said a voice from within. *He's just like the others. Kill him now while he's down.*

I lurched forward, intent on doing just that. Kneeling, I reached out and found myself brushing back his dark hair from his forehead. Passed out like this, the hard mask had transformed into an innocence that I found difficult to ignore.

What was going on here? This man—this creature, who I believed to be a shadowman—had just saved me. Then, with his dying breath, he had tried to send me to safety.

He'd even used a subtle psychic push, which would have worked on a human.

But I was no human.

I had to think fast, and more than that, I had to act fast. The amount of noise we'd just made in our quick fight would surely send some curious bystander to investigate. From my belt, I unhooked a small vial, popped the top, and brought it to the man's lips. It was a fast-acting poison, quick and painless. A fast death was the least I could do since he'd attempted to help.

I began to tip the vial upward, then hesitated. There was something strange at work here, and it prevented me from finishing him off.

With a frustrated groan, I rose to my feet, pacing away several steps before turning back with something akin to a growl. "Fine. I'll get you to safety, but after that, my debt will be repaid—and it will be open season."

Winding a quick spell over the two bodies to cover them from view, I placed a glamour on myself. It was a neat trick I'd learned—now, when I went in to speak with Dorin, he wouldn't see the bloody face or bruises that had just begun to form. I would be in pristine condition.

Stalking back to the tavern, I popped inside and found everyone in much the same position as before. Either they'd not heard the noise, or they simply didn't care. It was a mystery I didn't have time for at the moment.

"Dorin, I'm not feeling well. Would you be able to handle it on your own?"

"Sure thing, Arie," he said, using the nickname I preferred over my real name. "Feel better."

"Thanks." I tipped my lips up in a smile, grabbed my jacket, and slipped back out the door.

Placing the bomber over my arm, I approached the protection bubble containing my two problems and thought through my options. One, I would need to dispose of the dead shadowman's body. Two, I would need to find a safe place for the other man to heal—and somewhere I would have control once he woke.

I needed to know what, exactly, he was. He didn't seem wholly evil like the others, but there was still a darkness in him I didn't trust. He had saved my life, though, so I owed him this much.

Dropping the jacket to the ground, I closed my eyes and pulled myself inward, giving over to the weightless feeling that always happened between shifts. First, I became molecules so tiny I transformed into the air itself, allowing my clothes to bunch up unscathed. Then I rebuilt, pushing each atom back into place until I shimmered into the form of a large, predatory bird.

Gripping the shadowman by his repulsive shoulders with my sharp talons, I lifted him into the air, leaving the protective shield around the second man. He would be safe there until I could return. Any human that happened to walk down the alley wouldn't be able to see his body and would find themselves diverted around the space without being any the wiser.

I didn't go far, finding a piece of mountainside with a clearing large enough to build a fire. It was a distasteful task but a necessary one. The evidence of shadowmen had to remain a secret.

Dropping the body into a heap, I landed on the ground on my own two feet. Whispering into my cupped palms, I waited for the fire to grow into a substantial ball before releasing it into the shadowman. The flames instantly took over, a loud shriek filling the night. I'd blocked the noise before building the fire, so I felt secure that no one in town could hear—or see the flames.

It didn't take long for the body to turn to ash, which I swept away with a light wind. The shadowman had done enough damage on this earth; his evil remains needn't be a part of it.

There was only one more thing left to do: heal the earth from the scorch of supernatural fire.

As I'd done earlier in the day, I pushed my hands into the soft loam, calling to her, asking for the richest soil to replace this tainted patch. When new shoots pushed their way through the dirt, I sank back onto my heels and wiped the sweat from my forehead.

That alone told me I was at my breaking point of energy. Sweat wasn't something my kind did.

I shifted back into a bird with a thought. Practice made perfect; when I first learned this ability, I was slow and sometimes not completely put together. A missing limb or rearranged face could make it difficult to move—or, more importantly, fight—so I practiced for days on end until it became second nature.

Banking high to catch the wind traveling back toward town, I sailed over the treetops, my predator's gaze sharp. Where there was one shadowman, there tended to be another. I wouldn't be caught off guard again.

The joy of flying didn't escape me, but too many other things prevented me from fully enjoying it. Like the strange man lying in the street, his blood soaking into the ground from the knife I'd stabbed into his back.

When I reached the alley, I circled twice, making sure I wouldn't be seen when I reappeared outside the protective shield. Dropping into a dive, I was seconds from faceplanting when I shifted into molecules and spread out inside the clothes on the ground. When I stood again in my natural form, I was fully dressed.

Shrugging on the bomber jacket, I scooped the unconscious man into my arms, watching his relaxed face for a moment before looking up to the sky. Tilting my head back, I called in the clouds that were hovering on the horizon. As the sky darkened with the threat of a storm, I turned and began to walk.

The rain that came would wash the remaining blood away.

Chapter 3

In the end, there was only one place I could bring the mysterious man who had saved my life. The small, one-room cabin I'd rented for the duration of my stay was nestled in the mountains, far enough from the village to be free of prying eyes.

I laid him carefully on the bed, as it was the only available surface large enough to fit his frame. For a moment, I studied his face, brushing his thick bangs away from his eyes once again. Thankfully, those sparkling gems were closed—they did strange things to my mind and body, and I didn't need to deal with that right now.

There was something different about this shadowman. He didn't have the same evil stench as the others I'd dealt with. In sleep, he seemed almost...peaceful. Innocent.

A trick. All shadowmen were evil. I would do well to remember that.

Though I was short of blood, I did cover the man with thick blankets to keep him warm. Our kind could heal most wounds, given enough time to rest. The influx of blood was extremely helpful but not necessary.

He would survive, and it would give me time to figure out what, exactly, I was going to do with him. While I pondered that, I bound his hands and feet in a spell, using the strongest magic I possessed. Next, I put a bubble of protection over him—not only could no one else see him, but he also couldn't call out. Every shadowman had different abilities, and I couldn't take the risk that his was telepathy. The last thing I wanted was an army of shadowmen swooping down on my temporary home.

Done with ensuring his imprisonment, I stepped into the small bath and peeled off my clothing, filling the tub with cold water. I missed having hot showers but found I enjoyed relaxing in a tub after a fight. I didn't bother with using up the little bit of hot water I was able to coax out of the tap—not when I could produce fire.

When the water looked deep enough, I placed both hands inside and murmured another spell. The water began to heat instantly, and once it was the right temperature, I slipped into it with a grateful sigh. Sweeping my long hair up and over the edge to keep it dry for the time being, I closed my eyes and allowed the heat to penetrate every sore muscle. This was about relaxing and cleaning off the stench of evil. It was about planning my next steps.

Once the creature woke, I would question him and find out where he came from and how many others were in the area. Then, I would make sure to knock him out again with a spell that would wear off over time. If we ever met again, I would not be so lenient.

This would be the last day I spent in the small village I'd grown quite fond of. In the morning, before the creature woke, I would find the owners of the tavern and let them know I would not be back. It wasn't always a courtesy I was able to give, but I preferred to do so. I hated leaving good people in a lurch.

Feeling better with the semblance of a plan, I drained the tub and got dressed.

It was going to be a long night.

∞ ∞ ∞

THE SUN SHONE BRIGHTLY THROUGH the western window when the creature's eyes finally fluttered open. I sat in a chair beside the bed, watching him, knowing he would wake soon. We were both silent as his eyes finally met mine—me because I wanted him to understand his predicament and him because I'd spelled his vocal cords.

Though I'd expected him to glare, I was surprised to see he watched me with more curiosity than anger. More kindness than hate. It was unnerving. Using English, I said, "You are under my control. Do you speak English? Two blinks for yes."

He blinked twice.

"I will ask you questions. You will blink twice for yes, three times for no. Understand?" Two blinks again. At least he cooperated. "Are there others of your kind nearby?"

Three blinks.

"Were you working with the shadowman that attacked me?"

His eyes tightened, looked pained. Three blinks.

"All right, I'm going to allow you to speak. You can only answer my questions. Anything else, and I'll cut you off. Understand?"

Two blinks.

Releasing him, I waited to see if he would speak out of turn. He didn't. "Why are you here?"

He cleared his throat before speaking. "I am hunting a shadowman that killed my parents."

That was the last thing I expected him to say. He was *hunting* a shadowman? It must be a trick. "What did you do to the one that attacked me?"

There was a pause before he answered. "I am able to inflict pain on another with my mind."

Fear skittered along my skin. That was a powerful ability, indeed. I had to be very careful with this creature. I should kill him now and be done with it. But I couldn't. I'd made a promise. "I'm allowing you to live to repay my debt to you. If we ever cross paths again, I will not hesitate to kill you."

"A question then, before you release me."

My eyebrows drew together at his strange request. "Fine. One question."

"Tell me your name." My eyes searched his, looking for the hidden meaning behind his question. Could he somehow use my name against me? Could he track me with it or use it to release himself from my spells? It wasn't worth the risk. "My name is Emerson Drake. I see you're hesitant in telling me yours, and I understand. You believe I'm a shadowman, don't you?"

"And I suppose you'll tell me you're not?"

"I'm not," he insisted. "I'm an Elemental. Shadowmen are created when an Elemental gives into the darkness. I have not."

"Enough," I said sharply, waving a hand to re-enact the spell to cut off his voice. "I've never come across your so-called Elementals. All creatures with this power are evil and need to be destroyed."

Shoving back the chair as I stood, I glared down at the prone man. His story was ridiculous, and I was letting my emotions get the better of me. I needed time to think away from his probing eyes.

"I'll be back," I growled, spinning toward the door and slamming it behind me. In an instant, I transformed, my clothes remaining in a heap at the door.

Choosing the form of a lynx, needing to feel the earth below my feet, I sprang into the deep woods of the mountain. Lynx were indigenous to the area, though rarely seen. Their agile limbs worked perfectly in the untamed mountainous terrain.

I leaped easily across streams and gorges, using the powerful back legs of the beautiful creature I mimicked. Though the lynx typically had a top speed of forty miles per hour, I was able to use my preternatural speed in any form. Right now, I needed to feel the rush of wind against my fur and the soft earth beneath my paws.

In my mad race to be away from the creature I held hostage, I emptied my mind as I allowed the pent-up energy to dissipate. Only when I felt that wild compulsion abate did I slow and shuffle the information around in my mind.

If what this creature—Emerson—said was true, there might be others out there who were not evil. There was a small part of me, long ago buried, wanting to believe that with every fiber of my being. That small part was the remnant of a girl who had been murdered the day shadowmen took me, killed my brother, and changed me to be like them.

To be inherently evil.

What Emerson spoke of seemed too good to be true. This creature would obviously say anything to trick me, to get me to let my guard down. He was evil, he was powerful, and he was cunning. Letting him live had been a mistake. I needed to return now and take care of the problem once and for all.

Decision made, I slid to a halt and reversed direction. The sun began to make its final descent beneath the horizon, bathing the area in a golden hue. Dusk was the prelude to night; my time.

But not just my time. Other creatures began to emerge from their caves and hidey holes, seeking prey. Life was a constant struggle for survival, for man and beast alike. Of course, I fit more into the second category than the first.

Spotting a small pack of lynx, I huffed a greeting, letting them know I was a friendly, and we ran together along their territory. For a brief moment in time, I wasn't alone. I had a pack, a family. Then, they veered off, spotting a meal. I continued on my way, knowing I needed to return and deal with my problem.

Little did I know a larger one brewed just beyond the next stream.

The stench of evil hit me hard, but I didn't have time to slow down. In the next instant, a trap sprung. Razor wire cut through my back leg, stringing me upside down. My weight was supported only by a tree limb; haunting laughter spread across my mind.

"Where are you going, little cat?" a man's voice asked, leaving the feeling of oily slime along my skin.

Hissing in response, I quickly thought through my options. The first thing I'd attempted to do was shift, but the barbs inserted into my calf must have been spelled, for I was unable to. While part of my brain worked out the magic, I watched the approaching shadowman with hate in my eyes.

You're in trouble, came a voice from inside my mind. Startled, I held my breath, terrified by what that meant.

How are you doing this? I asked of Emerson. I would recognize his husky voice anywhere, even in the unlikely place of my mind.

You have need of me. Release me, and I will come to you.

Another trick. Emerson must be working with this new shadowman. He'd found a way around my spells to get a message out. I never should have left him alone.

Or alive.

Woman, you'll be the death of me, he muttered. *Tell me how to undo the spells.*

Why? I spat back, anger vibrating out from every cell of my body. *So you can come help your friend? Leave me alone. I'll deal with this, and then I'll come deal with you.*

Silence met my request. Perfect.

My attention now only split between two things—the shadowman who was watching me with triumph clear on his face and the spell he'd used to hold me in the form of the lynx.

The shadowman before me reached out to stroke my face. "I've been searching for you for a long time." With a hiss, I snapped at his hand, missing by millimeters. He pulled back quickly, a smirk on his face. "Glad to see you've got some fight in you. Would be boring otherwise."

He snapped his fingers, and I fell, hitting the ground hard. Exhaling a huff of breath, I struggled to stand, favoring my back leg. Whatever he'd done affected more than my shifting ability. For the first time in many years, I could taste my fear as the shadowmen wove his hands once more. Already, I felt myself freezing in place, my limbs useless and voice diminished in animal form.

This was the end, then. I welcomed it, accepted it. My existence was only good for one thing: taking out shadowmen. I'd vowed to myself long ago I would never be a hostage again.

He would never take me alive.

I felt a low rumbling beneath my paws, a heartbeat greater than any lifeform on the face of the earth. It was the earth itself calling out to me. Promising a safe haven. Offering shelter in the storm. As a last-ditch effort, I sent my thoughts into the ground. Though I normally dug my hands into the soil and murmured aloud, I willed Mother Earth to hear my call one last time.

Mother Earth, strong and true. Help your daughter, heed my call. Lend me your strength, send me your strongest brew. Break this spell so I can win this brawl.

The earth shuddered, long fissures snaking out from where my paws were planted firmly in the ground. The shadowman gasped and began to retreat, but he moved too slowly. Stumbling back, he fell against a hard, dark form, topped by a face blazing with fury.

Two strong, capable hands wrapped around the shadowman's jaw and snapped his neck with one quick twist. Tossing him aside, Emerson then fixed his gaze on me.

The spell broken thanks to the unexpected help of Mother Earth, I transformed back into my own form. The earth provided me with natural fibers woven into the shape of a long shirt to help cover me, so at least I didn't have to face this powerful creature nude.

Emerson and I stared at each other across the expanse of cracked and open earth, words escaping me. For the first time, he looked truly angry—but, underlying that, the unmistakable look of relief was evident.

"How did you escape?" I finally managed to ask, sorting through the events to zoom in on the most important question.

In a split-second, Emerson stood less than a foot away, towering over me. His emerald eyes glittered with so many emotions I couldn't pinpoint any of them. "You were in trouble and did not allow me to assist you. I had no choice but to break your spells."

"How is that possible?" I asked, fear and anger warring for supremacy. Anger at myself for losing my focus and allowing myself to be captured. Anger at Emerson for being good enough to break my magic. Anger at the shadowmen as a whole for existing.

More than that, an unrelenting fear of not only Emerson's innate power but the sudden realization of his power over me.

"I appreciate that you have no reason to trust me or to believe a word I say, but I cannot tell you an untruth." He took a deep breath, his hands twitching to reach out to me but resisting the urge. "You are my mate."

Wincing, I took several steps back, needing space between us. Mate. What every shadowman wanted. The reason I was hunted. "I'm no one's mate. Now, tell me how you were able to speak into my mind and how you were able to break through my spells. No other has done such a thing."

"I've already told you," Emerson responded calmly, knowing better than to approach me again. "We are mates. I am an Elemental, not a shadowman. We are connected in ways that neither of us can even imagine. Mates are able to speak telepathically, as are twins. Even though I couldn't reach out to my brother through your spell, I believe I was still able to reach you because you were the one who cast it."

"No," I said, shaking my head in denial. "No way. None of this is real. The only creatures I've ever come across that haven't been human have been evil. Every single one. I would have run across your kind before if what you say is true."

"There are few of us left. I'm sorry for what you've been through. It was obviously traumatizing, and I hope one day you trust me enough to tell me about it. But I am not evil, and I would never do anything to harm you. I am incapable."

My hands shook with trepidation. That small part of me, the one that had been long buried, struggled to believe his words. It sounded too good to be true. A group of decent people—Elementals. I didn't have to be alone anymore.

Then it hit me. Of course I would be alone. Even if what Emerson said was true, *I* wasn't good. There was evil stamped into my very soul. I couldn't be near humans or this mythical group of Elementals for very long.

"You're mistaken." I spoke in a whisper, unshed tears poised to spill. "Even if what you say is true, I can't be your mate."

He cocked his head to the side. "What do you mean?"

"It doesn't matter. I still think you're a shadowman. A clever one, for sure, but evil just the same."

Emerson sighed but had yet to lose his cool with me. Even earlier, when he'd disabled the shadowman with a twist of his wrist, he'd been furious—but not really at me.

Holding out a palm, Emerson created a ball of fire and tossed it casually into the shadowman behind him. The body went up in flames, that same eerie shriek assaulting my ears. It lasted just a few moments until Emerson dispersed the ashes with a thought.

That repugnant task done, he turned his attention back to me, his eyes thoughtful. When he spoke, his tone was light, conversational. As if the subject matter weren't of vital importance. "The earth refuses to speak to shadowmen. As Elementals, we are closely connected to the earth and all the elements. Giving up one's soul means giving up the fundamental parts of oneself."

Here he knelt, slipped his fingers into the soil. I watched him warily, uncertain what his endgame was. "Do you trust her?" Emerson asked. "Do you trust Mother Earth?"

"Of course," I murmured.

"Kneel. Speak to her. Ask her if you can trust me."

Staring at him for several beats of time, I finally took a deep breath and knelt on the ground. The dried blood on my calf made itself known with a crinkling sound though the wound had closed. Emerson caught sight of it, his eyes narrowing, but he said nothing.

Digging my hands into the earth, I closed my eyes and first thanked her for saving me. I felt the pulse there, the unrelenting beat that told me the earth was alive and well. "Mother Earth, creator of life. Your son and daughter are here to relieve your strife. Heal your wounds and cleanse above all. In your name, heed our call."

Tendrils of heat flowed between Emerson's hands and mine, the earth connecting the three of us together. A moment of perfect understanding and clarity flowed over and around us as the fissures healed and the wind swirled leaves in gentle eddies. My hair lifted, caught in the playful dance, as my eyes rose to meet Emerson's.

Our gazes locked together as the earth revealed our truths. His soul laid bare before me; he hid nothing from my gaze. His aura was the softest yellow, like a winter's dawn—brightest in the area of his heart and darkening around the edges to a golden wheat color.

I gasped with the beauty of it, never having seen anything so pure since I'd been turned into the creature I was. So enraptured by its beauty, I didn't notice the look on his face at first.

Horror began in his eyes and transformed his features until his mouth formed a perfect O. I realized my soul shined as clear to him as his to me. Glancing down, wanting to see what he saw, I discovered that what had previously been a rich, soil-like hue now bore ebony blotches strewn haphazardly across its surface. Moreover, I realized that the majority of the aura undulating around me had turned dark—and evil.

Shadowed.

Springing back from my crouched position, I lost my connection to the earth and, through her, to Emerson. The wind instantly died down as his aura faded from view.

"Wait—" he began, but I didn't allow him to finish.

Shaking my head, for the second time that day, I turned and ran away.

Chapter 4

Remaining in my true form, I raced across the ground as fast as my feet allowed. They barely scratched the earth as I flew, my heart pounding in my chest as I pushed myself to the limit. The wind whipped through my long hair, and my eyes narrowed in determination. I was in a battle against what lay behind me—a threat I couldn't quite comprehend—and myself, my own fears and doubts threatening to overtake me. But I couldn't let them win. I had to keep going, had to find a way to outrun the danger that nipped at my heels. My immortal life depended on it.

Please, talk to me, came the voice inside my head. I didn't respond. I had no response. The look on his face had said it all. *Please. I don't even know your name.*

And it would stay that way. I had to leave this place, start anew. The few belongings I possessed would have to remain behind. It wouldn't be the first time, and it wouldn't be the last. It would take me a while to replenish the small arsenal I had and the specialty clothing I'd designed for fighting—but if there was one thing I had, it was plenty of time.

My warning systems went into overdrive. I was being followed. Before I could react, two arms of steel wrapped around my waist, and I flew toward the ground. We rolled several times, though I barely felt a jolt or a scratch. Emerson wrapped his arms around my head and protected me from the fall—though, as he was the reason we were tumbling to begin with, I wasn't giving him any extra points for chivalry.

We landed with an oomph, my back against the hard ground while Emerson straddled me. Instincts had me fighting, but he wrapped my wrists into one strong hand while his eyes gleamed down at me. "Please stop struggling. I will not hurt you; I only wish to talk."

"Let me go," I hissed, refusing to cease my fight.

"I don't want to force you, woman. Please don't make me."

Pausing my struggles for a moment, I glared up at him. "You won't take me alive."

His face went lax; I could see the pity in his eyes. That was the last thing I wanted from anyone. When he spoke, his voice went so soft, so gentle, it was nearly my undoing. "What happened to you?"

"Bastards like you, that's what happened. Now let me go."

Surprisingly, he released my wrists as if he'd been burned. He sprang back, and I crouched, prepared for whatever attack he had planned. "I will not force you to do anything; I only wish to speak with you. Prove to you what I say is true. Would you grant me that?"

"You've seen what I am, and I've seen what you truly think of me."

"No. What you saw on my face was not because of you but what has been done to you." For a moment, my heart stilled in my chest. Actually skipped a beat, like in some stupid, sappy romantic comedy. It was absurd how much I wanted to believe in what he said. "Please, just speak with me for a little while. You don't have to tell me your name if you don't wish me to know. I will keep my distance. I just want to get to know you."

My senses flared out, though my gaze remained steady on his ridiculously handsome face. Through the earth, I knew where each animal, large or small, was located. I could hear every scratch of claws against trees, every flap of wings. When I inhaled, I could catch any scent—including Emerson's. He smelled of a deep musk with a surprising underlying flowery scent—peony or lilac—as if he'd been running in wolf form through a field of flowers.

Rising slowly to my feet, I left my senses on high alert but gave in to that small voice I'd been pushing aside for so long. I spoke to him. "You said you have a twin."

Relief instantly washed over his features, but he was careful to remain at a distance. With a nod, he answered, "Yes, Dominic. He's been in America, though he plans on joining me here. We've both been searching for the shadowman who killed our parents."

"So...you were born like this?" I asked, trying to piece together the things he'd told me.

"Yes. Elementals are born but can also be made. If someone is Gifted, they have the ability to be converted."

Wincing again, I answered lowly, "I know."

"Is that what happened to you? Were you converted by a shadowman?"

Swallowing hard, I nodded. Admitted my ultimate shame. "Yes."

I could feel the waves of fury rolling off him, though again, it wasn't directed toward me. Watching him curiously, I saw his features shift into a mask of calm. The rage hovered there, behind his eyes, but his face relaxed. "I'm so sorry for what you've been through. Shadowmen are evil creatures that need to be expunged from this world."

"At least that's something we can agree on. I've been hunting them since...since I escaped."

"Alone? You've been hunting shadowmen alone?"

Shrugging, I gestured around me. "I had no other choice."

Having to calm himself again, Emerson waited to speak until the anger dissipated. "Would you like to get some dinner?" Startled by his change of topic, I instantly began to search the mountainside, wary. "We can go to a public place. I haven't eaten or fed since before we first met—and I know you haven't, either. It would be my pleasure to take you to dinner."

"I'm leaving this place," I said, raising my chin. "I've already quit my job."

"It's just dinner," he said, his lips turning up at the corner. I found my gaze suddenly riveted to his mouth. "And if, after that, you still want nothing to do with me—I'll leave you be."

Glancing down, I realized I still only wore a long shirt the earth had fashioned for me. If I agreed, I could go home, pack my few belongings. Have dinner with this strange creature and then leave.

"Just dinner," I emphasized. Once he nodded affirmation, I agreed. "All right. But I need to go home and put on clothes."

"Of course," he said, gesturing with a hand. "After you."

Before I could change my mind, I put on a burst of speed, racing toward the small cabin I'd become quite fond of in my time here. Emerson stayed beside me, keeping his distance, which I appreciated. I was still wary of him and his speed—he'd caught me all too easily before, and that irked me. Slowing as I reached the small lawn, I glanced over at Emerson. "Stay here."

"As you wish." He smiled fully, and I sucked in a breath at the transformation of his face. After a beat too long, I went inside and quickly gathered my most treasured items into a backpack before dressing in my usual attire of black leather. The belt went on my hips, and I filled the arsenal from my supply. When I glanced in the mirror, I realized my hair had become a tangled mess, though the bruising on my face had already healed.

Wanting to look presentable—not for Emerson, of course, but for anyone we ran into—I dragged a brush through my hair and deftly braided it, giving me a semblance of control over the wild strands. After splashing some cold water on my face to deal with the worst of the dirt, I took a deep breath and left the tiny room.

Stepping out of the door, I found Emerson waiting with a fistful of flowers. They were peonies, which only brought out his own scent stronger than before. I glared at him with arms crossed. "You moved."

He shrugged, relentless. "Just for a moment. A woman should have flowers before a date."

"What century are you from?" I asked in a snarky tone. He threw me off, and I didn't like it. Not one bit.

"The late twentieth," he responded with that same sexy grin. "I'm as old as I look."

"Hm," I grunted, reaching out to take the small bundle from his hands. "They do smell good."

His smile was still prevalent as he offered his arm. "Shall we?"

Staring at his elbow with no small amount of disgust, I slipped both straps of the backpack over my shoulders and started forward, using a human pace. Emerson didn't seem deterred by my standoffishness; if anything, he seemed to get more jovial as time went on.

He also seemed content to follow at my slow pace, keeping up a stream of easy conversation as we walked. "Where are you from?"

"I was born in Australia," I said, finding no harm in it. "You?"

"America. A small town in Iowa," he replied. "Ever been to America?"

"I've been everywhere. I don't stay anywhere for very long."

"Sounds lonely," he commented, and I could feel his eyes on me.

"It's the only life I can live."

"Do you have any family?"

My hands tightened into fists as the onslaught of emotions slammed into me. "No."

Registering the clipped answer, Emerson knew better than to go any further down that path. "What's your favorite food?"

"Food is food. Blood is blood. It's just sustenance."

Here, he stopped, forcing me to pause in order to avoid a collision. His eyes met mine, searching even as he spoke softly. "You weren't always like this. Don't you remember what life was like before this darkness took over? How good it can be?"

My eyes tightened with pain. "That's not my reality anymore. Why should I torture myself with something that can't be?"

"I hope, someday soon, that you can move on from the darkness."

Without another word, he turned and continued toward the only restaurant in town. I followed him hesitantly, wondering if I should just turn around and go anywhere else. My bag was packed. I was ready. He reached the door and looked back, his beautiful eyes watching me. I felt inexplicably drawn to this strange man and knew, somewhere deep down, that I was in a profound amount of trouble.

With one foot in front of the other, I approached the restaurant—and the dangerous man who wouldn't take his eyes off me.

The restaurant was attached to the inn, and when I reached the door, Emerson opened it. I kept a close eye on him as I entered the room, still waiting for the other shoe to drop. While I believed that he wasn't like the other shadowmen I'd come across, I still didn't trust his intentions.

I chose a table in the corner where I could easily see the room and both exits. Emerson sat across from me, though I could tell he would normally prefer not to turn his back on a room. It was his way of showing me his trust, I supposed. It didn't matter. After this one dinner, I was gone.

Maria greeted us, bringing over glasses of water and a basket of bread with fresh butter. She was the daughter of the innkeeper and had been running the restaurant since she'd turned eighteen.

"Good evening, Arie," she said as she set the water down. I cringed, realizing Emerson had just learned my name—nickname though it was.

"Good evening, Maria. What is Danut making tonight?" I asked her in Romanian. Danut was the chef, and apart from the small menu, he always had a chef's special.

"Beef stew and papanasi for dessert."

"We'll take two of those," I said with a smile, then looked over at Emerson. He seemed content to let me order and seemed oblivious to the shy glances Maria sent him. Some tendril of an emotion I couldn't name spread from my chest to my stomach, but I forced myself to ignore it.

"Arie, is it?" Emerson asked once we were alone.

"Don't look so smug. It's a nickname."

"At least I have something to call you," he returned, not seeming in the least bothered.

"How long have you been in Romania?"

He didn't comment on my abrupt subject change. "Two weeks. I've been tracking shadowmen across Europe but have yet to find the one I'm looking for."

"Do you know his name?"

"No." Emerson seemed frustrated by this fact. "Only his scent. My brother and I...we found our parents shortly after their death. The shadowman was gone, but his stench remained."

In his anger, I felt an unexpected connection to him. Picking up a piece of bread and slathering it with the butter, I took a bite while I digested what he'd told me. Deciding there was no harm in being polite, I finally said, "I'm sorry about your parents. I know what it's like to lose those you love."

"Who did you lose?"

With a sigh, I decided to answer him this time. "My parents when I was young. Then my brother."

"That's terrible," he said, reaching across the table as if to clasp my hand. It rested there, just out of reach. "I couldn't imagine not having my brother."

"Why is he not with you now?"

"We got two different leads at the same time. He followed one to Minnesota, in America, while I followed one to Europe. He...he met his mate and almost lost her to a shadowman. They were delayed in traveling here."

There was that word again. Mate. "And you think I'm your mate. Why?"

He watched me intently as he answered. "Though we didn't grow up with others of our kind, our parents taught us everything they knew about Elementals. The language, the legends, everything. There is an undeniable connection between mates—I know you feel it, too, even if you don't recognize what it is—plus, we are able to speak telepathically. As I've said before, only twins and mates have that ability."

"I don't feel anything," I denied. "Plus, some shadowmen are able to speak telepathically to anyone."

"I don't have that ability. You've seen mine. Also, you do feel something." Maria returned with steaming bowls of thick stew, smiling shyly at Emerson before leaving. I tracked her with squinted eyes. "Like that."

His words forced my gaze back to him. "Like what?"

"You're feeling jealous because Maria is showing me attention."

"That's the most ridiculous thing I've ever heard."

"All right then, why didn't you kill me last night? I was unconscious and near death. You could have finished me off. What stopped you?"

"I—well, I still might," I said with a glare. "Anyway, I made a promise. A life for a life. I owed you that much."

"Would you have saved any other man you thought was a shadowman?"

"No other shadowman ever attempted to help me."

"Exactly. But it's more than that, and I know you know it."

Shaking my head, I took a bite of the stew. The heat slid down my throat, and the thick chunks filled my stomach. "I don't know."

"Then I'll continue to prove it to you until you believe me."

Our eyes met in a battle of wills. He was strong, but I'd been honed in the very fires of hell. If anything, he'd met his match. Maria appeared, refilling our glasses of water, and we both sat back. Neither of us gave in or surrendered. It wasn't in our nature.

As Maria walked away, I had the startling realization that I may have met *my* match.

"The stew is delicious," Emerson commented, taking another spoonful.

"Yes, it is," I agreed, still reeling.

The stew was indeed delicious, but my mind was far from the food. I couldn't stop thinking about what Emerson had said—that I was his mate. It was a ridiculous notion, one I couldn't even begin to entertain. I'd spent too many years alone, fighting for my life and the lives of others. I couldn't afford to let anyone in, especially not someone who claimed to be my soulmate.

And yet...there was something about him that drew me in. I would never admit it to him, but it was the way he looked at me, the way he spoke to me—it was as if he saw past all the walls I'd built up over the years.

Using a piece of bread to sop up the last of the liquid, I sat back with my arms crossed to study my companion. He had awakened something deep inside me, something I hadn't ever felt, even as a human. Attraction.

For a long time, I'd thought something had been wrong with me. I was never interested in boys, not like the other girls in school. I had always searched for the next adventure, some uncharted territory. I didn't have time for relationships then, and I didn't now. I knew what my life was, what my purpose was.

And I wholly expected not to live through it.

Even if I believed Emerson, what kind of future could we have? There was no future for us. It would be better if he understood that now before he became too attached.

Maria cleared our bowls and replaced them with a towering stack of cheese donuts with fresh smetana and a blueberry sauce drizzled over the top.

"Wow, these look wonderful," Emerson said to Maria, surprising me by speaking Romanian. "Multumesc."

She blushed and asked if we needed anything else. When Emerson shook his head, she hurried away. Cutting into the pastry, I muttered, "You're going to give her an aneurism."

"I was just being polite."

After I'd shoved a bite into my mouth, I looked up to find his gaze on me. It was unnerving. "What?"

"You're beautiful," he answered simply. Swallowing the bite of pastry, I felt horribly self-conscious. "Whether your eyes are spitting fire at me, or you're enjoying a dessert, or fighting a shadowman. You're beautiful."

Clearing my throat, I forked another bite instead of answering him. How was I supposed to answer something like that? Emerson remained quiet also, trying the dessert for himself. I ate quickly, reminding myself that the sooner this dinner was over, the sooner I could be on my way.

"Romania certainly has amazing food," Emerson said, finally breaking the silence.

"I like it."

"Have you tried the cabbage rolls?"

"Sure." I shrugged. "Danut makes big batches on the weekend."

"They're unlike any I've ever had before."

"It's the sour cabbage. Makes all the difference."

"And apple strudel," Emerson continued. "Best in the world."

Shrugging again, I ate the last of my dessert. "I guess so."

"You want to leave."

"I do," I said. There was no point denying it.

"Where will you go?" Pressing my lips into a thin line, I stared at him. With a half-smile, he answered that himself. "You don't want me to know. I understand."

"I'd like to cover a good distance before dawn." Pulling money from my bag, I began to place enough Lei on the table to cover the meals when Emerson held up his hand.

"No, this is my treat. I asked you to dinner; it's the least I can do." Hesitating briefly, I finally nodded before stuffing it back into the pack. Standing, I slung the bag across my shoulder and paused when Emerson stood with me. "Please, before you leave—at least tell me your real name."

Distrust was heavy in my gaze. Emerson nodded in defeat. "Then allow me to walk you out."

"Fine," I grumbled, heading for the door. Whatever it took to be on my way. We walked out of town and into the foothills covered by woods. I took a last look back at the tiny village that had been my home for the last month, realizing I would miss it.

"Please...be safe. I understand you feel the need to hunt these creatures, but you don't have to do it alone. If at any time you need me, I'm just a call away." Emerson discreetly tapped his temple in a reminder of our connection.

Without a word, I nodded, then turned and began to walk away. After only a few steps, I hesitated and looked back at him. He remained rooted to the spot, his eyes heavy on mine. With a deep breath, I finally gave him what he wanted.

"Aurelia," I said. "My name is Aurelia."

Chapter 5

With every step that carried me further from Emerson, it seemed as though I left a tiny piece of my soul in my wake. Hardening myself against the temptation to turn and see where these new feelings could lead, I began to run. Escape was my only thought, first and foremost. Where I headed or when I would stop didn't matter.

I just needed to leave.

As I encountered one scattered village after another, I gave them a wide berth, unprepared to interact with anyone quite yet. It was only once the terrain turned mountainous again and the sky brightened with the first vestiges of day that I finally ceased my flight.

I'd been running north, and my best guess at my location was somewhere still in the Carpathian Mountains but near the Ukraine border. The tiny village nestled near the Ceahlău National Park would be my home for the day.

I would eat, and I would plan.

Heading for the only inn the town possessed, I cast a glamour and walked inside. With a deep breath, I approached the front desk to ask for a room. A kind-looking woman who introduced herself as Cristina greeted me and showed me upstairs. She didn't seem to find it strange that I came in near dawn looking for a place to stay, and I appreciated her discretion. The room was small but had its own bath, for which I paid extra.

"Would you like some breakfast?" she asked.

Though I'd eaten with Emerson, my run had taken precious energy. I also had not fed in a few days, but that would have to wait. Setting my bag down near the bed, I answered her, "Da, multamusc."

She smiled and disappeared down the hall, so I made a quick check of ingress points before she returned. I would easily be able to protect the room but liked to know its weaknesses—and my exit plan—in case something, or someone, got through my safeguards.

Cristina returned shortly with a covered plate on a tray. After thanking her again, she left me alone to eat. On the plate were several mici, which were a spiced combination of meat shaped like sausages, with boiled potatoes and freshly made bread. Slipping a few sausages into one of the rolls, I slathered on some mustard and ate it like a sandwich, my stomach rumbling in anticipation.

Though it wasn't as flavorful as Danut's had been, they were still delicious and, more importantly, satisfying.

Once finished with the meal, I set the tray aside and pulled open the bag I'd brought with me. My short trip back to the cabin I'd been renting gave me time to grab some of the essentials—such as my weapons belt, extra poison I'd cultivated, and most items from the small arsenal I'd collected. Sitting on top, where I'd stuffed them on entering the restaurant with Emerson, were the flowers he'd given me, now wilted and past drooping.

I picked them up, intending to toss them in the trash, but my fingers brushed lightly over them instead. Taking a few of the least damaged, I spread the petals gently open and pressed them into one of the books I'd brought with me. It was a stupid thing, but it wasn't the flowers' fault that I wanted nothing to do with Emerson.

Settling back with a different book, I set in for a long day. I had to spend the day inside, as was my curse. The sunlight didn't agree with my skin, so I avoided it when I was able—like a vampire from fiction.

The day passed slowly as I tried to distract myself with the book. But not matter how engaging the story was, my mind kept drifting back to Emerson and the time we'd spent together. I replayed our conversations, dissecting every word and gesture for hidden meanings. Could he really be what he said? Or was he truly a shadowman?

I sighed and set the book aside, unable to concentrate. Restless energy thrummed through my body, urging me to move, to do something, but I was trapped inside until nightfall.

Needing to occupy myself with something physical, I sorted through my weapons again, checking each one for any damage or wear. The routine was soothing, the familiarity of it calming my nerves. As I worked, my thoughts gradually quieted, allowing me to focus on the task at hand.

Once I finished, I moved on to my clothes, folding and refolding the few items with precise, measured movements. The monotony of it lulled me into a meditative state, and for a little while, I was able to forget about Emerson and the complicated tangle of emotions he evoked.

But as the day turned to night, my anxiety returned. I needed to be out, hunting, doing something to ease some of this bundle of nervous energy that sat like a weight in my belly. I checked my surroundings to make sure no one was around before raising the window. Most people in the village had turned in for the evening; this was a place of farmers and merchants, who rose with the sun and were early to bed. That suited my purposes perfectly.

Slipping out of the window, I used the air to lower myself to the ground, obscuring my image in case someone happened to look outside. As soon as my feet touched the earth, I began moving, using my unnatural speed to reach the base of the steep mountains.

The area was rich in history and lore, as Transylvania wasn't far, and the legend of Dracula still frightened children and fascinated adults. The elderly whispered of dark creatures to the children, warning them from certain areas of the countryside. Though they used these tales as a deterrent against the children wandering off on their own, there was still something to the stories.

Especially now, when I knew there were shadowmen nearby.

I could sense them, or perhaps it was the earth sending me signals. It was always difficult to tell what came from the earth and what was my own instincts, but I used the information just the same.

Heading slightly east, I cast out all my senses, searching for any sign of evil lurking in the shadows. It was fully dark now, a time when the shadowmen would be at their full strength. That didn't matter to me. Hunting them down was my only concern.

Deep into the trees, I paused, sensing something close. I felt an oily substance crawling over my skin, alerting me to a shadowman's proximity. Though I remained perfectly still, I listened intently for the slightest sound, watching for the slightest movement, inhaling for the slightest scent out of place. Their location was revealed to me through the soles of my feet.

In a practiced move, I spun, knife in my hand, and shot the weapon directly at the shadowman's throat. He dodged, though it scraped the side of his neck. I smiled grimly but was already on the move, shifting two more weapons from belt to hands.

"You will come with me, girl," the creature spat, but I ignored him and launched into an attack.

Blades sliced through the air as I swiped and spun, not giving the shadowman a moment's rest. He snarled and defended against the attacks, but I was relentless.

I moved in close, and ignoring the sharp blades, the shadowman wrapped his arms around my waist, trapping my arms beneath. At first, I struggled to release myself—then, when I began to dissolve into the air itself, he bit down in the crevice where neck meets shoulder.

Crying out with a little pain and a whole lot of disgust, I completed the shift and allowed the clothes to drop to the ground. In the next instant, I re-materialized inside them, already rolling to my feet.

Blood dripped from my wound, but I didn't bother to seal it. My healing powers would do that on their own.

"You'll pay for that," I said with a snarl, renewing my attack. I was a flurry of movements, which the shadowman tried valiantly to block. There wasn't a moment's pause in my actions as I began murmuring under my breath.

Material from the woods began collecting together—twigs, pine needles, leaves—and wrapped tightly in and around each other, forming a thick rope imbued with the strength of my magic. When enough of it fused together, it began to wrap around the shadowman, starting at his legs and spiraling up his torso until he found himself immobile.

Only then did I pause, just long enough to create fire in my hand, sending it into the creature's writhing form. He screamed curses at me, attempting to undo what I had done, but the trap had already been sprung.

He went up in flames, that same terrible shriek echoing across the ground. I quickly chanted for a sound barrier but knew I hadn't trapped it all. Any sound that emerged would merely be added to the myth of Dracula and these hills.

When the shadowman had been reduced to nothing more than a pile of ashes, I flicked a wrist to scatter the remains across the wind and finally knelt, my strength giving up. The wound had yet to close, and that told me the shadowman had done something to his teeth or his saliva—it didn't matter, but I needed to fix it before I bled out.

Mother Earth, strong and true. Send me herbs to seal this wound.

My hands were dug into the dirt, sending my urgent need through the earth. Small shoots began to spring up around me, and when they were fully grown, I picked them carefully, wrapping the comfrey root, rosemary, lavender, and geranium into a poultice to hold against my neck.

Sinking onto my butt to wait, I let out a deep sigh and took a good look around. The first knife I'd thrown had lodged into the trunk of a tree, which I would need to retrieve. A scorch mark stained the ground where the shadowman had burned, which I would need to heal. His oily aura remained evident in the air, needing to be cleansed. Even in my weakened state, I would make sure I left no trace of the vile creature. It was the least I could do for Mother Earth.

Once I felt the bleeding stop, I struggled to my feet and staggered toward the knife first. I knew it was dangerous to allow my energy to become this low, but there was nothing I could do about it at the moment.

Aurelia, came a strong voice. *You have pushed yourself too hard. Allow me to come to you.*

For a moment, I rested my forehead against the trunk of the tree, pushing away all emotion his voice invoked. He would get nothing but silence from me.

I'm only a call away, he said, his presence fading away.

Ignoring the strange curling sensation in the pit of my stomach, I removed the blade and murmured a healing chant for the bark. Next, I set to work on the ground, knowing it would take all of my remaining strength to fix what had been wrought.

Sinking down once again, I spoke the same whispered chant I always used to heal the earth. *Mother Earth, giver of life. Darkness has descended upon you, caused you strife. Send me sage, to cleanse this air. Send me copper; send me selenium; send me iodine; spread their richness for your ground to share. Dispel this evil once and for all; in your name, heed my call.*

As she sent the necessary herbs my way, I collapsed, at the end of my energy. I lay back, staring up at the night sky and trying to remember my reasons for continuing this existence.

Maurice is still out there, a tiny voice reminded me, as it always did. Still, for several minutes, I continued to lay, exhaustion overtaking me. Soon, I would move, I would return to the village, and I would allow my body the rest it needed.

Soon. The minutes turned into an hour, but I refused to get up, my limbs heavy and useless. As the first light of day streaked across the sky, I finally forced myself to my knees. Once there, it took only a little more effort to stand.

Leaning heavily against a tree, I focused my eyes on the distance, knowing I needed to walk at a human pace to make it back. My hunger had turned ravenous, and I was afraid of coming across a single human on my journey back. If I fed now, as starved as my cells were, I could easily lose control.

Taking my first steps forward, I stumbled my way through the woods on an unerring path back to town. Back to my room, where I could lay and allow myself to heal.

I lost track of how long it took to return, but the sun had moved well over the horizon by the time I climbed the stairs at the inn. Though the day had begun, and I'd spotted several humans moving about, I'd managed to avoid them as necessary.

I needed blood, but first, I needed to sleep.

Letting myself into the room, I dropped onto the bed, not bothering to remove the weapons or even my shoes. With the last shred of strength that I possessed, I set a barrier on the room, deterring any humans from entering—and killing any shadowmen that dared.

I can feel your exhaustion beating at me. Why don't you feed? Squeezing my eyes tight against the waves of relief rolling through me at hearing his voice again, I remained silent. Indulging in even light conversation with that man was dangerous—to me and to him. *I am here, if you have need of me.*

Shoving my face into a pillow, I struggled against emotions that had been long dead but seemed to be blossoming anew. How could the simple act of hearing his voice send butterflies racing in my stomach? His concern spread warmth across my chest?

Sleep was necessary, even though I knew what would happen. What always happened.

Against my better judgment, out of necessity, I closed my eyes and gave in to the darkness—and the dreams.

∞ ∞ ∞

ADEN!" SITTING UP WITH A start, I placed one hand against my pounding heart.

Aurelia? Are you all right?

How was it that he could be in my mind, feeling my emotions? Telepathy was only supposed to be a way to communicate. Emerson's capabilities felt so much more, so...intimate.

Shaking my head to clear all remnants of the same nightmare that haunted me every time I closed my eyes, I rolled to my feet and attempted to stand. Though my body had healed, my cells were still starved for blood. I knew I needed to feed, and soon. The hunger was a constant ache in my belly, growing more insistent with each passing minute.

Forcing myself upright, I stepped into the bathroom. A small bathtub awaited me, which I quickly filled with cool water. On the sink, I found a basket with toiletries, and I studied each carefully wrapped soap. It had been locally made with goat milk and lavender. The light scent instantly reminded me of Emerson with his oddly floral musk.

Though I hadn't answered Emerson, I could feel him hovering there, just outside my peripheral. An odd sensation at best—almost as if I was being watched, though not as unpleasant. It felt strangely comforting.

After heating the water, I sank into the tub and willed my body to relax. I would have to get a move on today toward my next destination, and I would have to find a way to feed.

It was late evening when I went down the stairs and found Cristina at the desk. My fangs lengthened when my eyes snagged on the pulsing vein in her neck, and I forced myself to breathe through it. After paying the woman for another night, even though I wouldn't be using the room, I ventured into the small restaurant to order food. A hearty meal would give me enough strength to find blood without terrifying the locals.

Ordering a stew, I waited at a barstool until it was delivered. There were large chunks of meat, potato, and other root vegetables, and I gulped it down quickly.

I asked the cook—who was the only employee in the place—where I could find a tavern. A tavern would have men, and though I preferred not to have alcohol-laced blood, their already fuzzy mindsets would be beneficial in my weakened state.

Leaving the inn, I ventured down the street, following the cook's direction. It didn't take long to find suitable targets—there were four men outside the tavern, perfect for my needs. Putting on a confused smile, I asked for help in Romanian and gestured around the back of the bar. They followed me, and this time, when I smiled, my fangs were on full display. The first man's eyes widened in terror, but in a flash, I had him pinned against the wall, one hand clamped over his mouth to muffle his cries. "Nu te voi răni," I whispered, taking control of his mind. I quickly wove a spell to mask all of their memories.

The first man relaxed in my grip as the others' expressions turned blank. My gaze snagged on the pulse in his throat, but I lifted his wrist instead. Taking blood from the neck felt too intimate. Without further thought, I sank my fangs into the flesh of his wrist and drank deeply. The blood was hot and sweet, and even in my weakened state, I was careful not to take too much. I drank from each man until I was full. They stared at me, dazed and confused, so I added one more compulsion while adding a bit of money to their pockets. "Du-te acasă. Uită că m-ai văzut vreodată."

They nodded slowly and stumbled off into the night, splitting off toward their individual homes as I'd requested. I watched them go, feeling the familiar mix of satisfaction and guilt that always accompanied feeding. No matter how many times I did it, I never quite got used to the necessity of taking blood from others.

Fully infused with proper energy, I set off at a run, not knowing my next destination. It didn't matter, anyway. I just had to keep moving.

∞ ∞ ∞

AFTER RUNNING ALL NIGHT, I found another small inn to rest for the day. Even though I was physically strong, I felt exhaustion beating at me. It was born from tiring of my existence more than the physical strain of running across countries.

Sinking against the single pillow on the twin-sized bed, I closed my eyes but willed myself to stay awake. Sleep helped to heal my wounds, but otherwise, it wasn't worth the emotional torture.

Good evening, came the silky voice. Placing the heel of my hand against my forehead, I applied pressure to relieve the insistent ache there. *My brother and his mate have joined me. They were delayed because Reese wasn't feeling well, and they were concerned her conversion hadn't gone well. It turns out that she's expecting. The babies went through the conversion with her. Though they're trying to hide it, I can see how worried they both are. This is not something any of us have heard of before.*

My heart jumped in my throat, and I recognized the emotion as anxiety for the woman I'd never met.

Reese is...spunky. She's not afraid to speak her mind, and she constantly puts Dominic in his place. It's rather refreshing to witness.

My lips twitched at the amusement in his voice before I even realized I'd reacted.

Reese is a writer, and she loves to explore. This is her first time in this area, though she told me she spent quite a bit of time in Europe. She's fascinated by the vampiric legends, of course. She's making us go on something called a Dracula Tour. The bafflement in his tone only made me smile. *I know you asked for space, and I am giving that to you, but I'd like to keep in contact. I think we'll both fare better that way. If you want me to stop, just say so.*

I remained silent, though I contemplated using the out he so gallantly offered me. But that would require responding, and I didn't want to do that, either.

Goodnight then, Aurelia.

Keeping my eyes closed, I took in one deep breath after another, using a meditation technique I'd come across on my constant travels. I'd found meditation worked as well as sleep for the days I wasn't wounded. It would rejuvenate my mind while my body rested.

But as I rested, my spirit drifted, the room as vivid in my subconscious as it had been in real life. The cement floor was cold and rough beneath my body, its unyielding surface offering no comfort. The metal bars that surrounded me were more than just physical barriers; they were imbued with dark magic, restraining my powers and rendering me helpless. I could feel the sinister energy emanating from them, a constant reminder of my captivity. The air was thick with the stench of despair and hopelessness, as if the very walls had absorbed the misery of those who came before me.

My entire body throbbed with pain, every muscle and joint screaming in agony as I lay in a crumpled heap on the cold, hard floor. I had been in this miserable position ever since Maurice had carelessly discarded me here, like a broken toy he no longer had any use for. It was becoming an almost daily occurrence now, his visits to my cell growing more frequent and more brutal with each passing day. He would drag me out, forcing his twisted will upon me, violating my body and mind with a sickening sense of entitlement. In his delusional state, he genuinely believed that these vile acts would somehow restore his fractured soul, as if my suffering could somehow atone for his own sins. But I knew better. His soul was lost, consumed by the darkness that had taken root within him long ago. There was no redemption to be found in my pain, no salvation waiting for him on the other side of my torment. He was a monster, pure and simple, and I was nothing more than a plaything for his perverse desires.

Every part of me was bruised or bleeding, inside and out. His attentions were beyond cruel. Tears leaked from the corners of my eyes, though I barely noticed. Noticing would have taken feeling, and I had none left.

"Arie," said a sweet voice from beside me. It was too much effort to turn my head, but my finger managed to twitch in acknowledgment. There was so much worry in her next words. "He is getting worse. If he does not let you heal, we will never get out of here."

"Edith," I rasped, barely loud enough for my own ears. "Go. You go."

"Not without you," she insisted. I felt a warm, gentle hand against my arm. Even though my skin shrieked in agony at the contact, I didn't want her to let go. "We are in this together, and we are getting out together."

Struggling to lift my lids, to peer at her beautiful face and the only source of hope in my dark existence, I managed to open them a crack. Edith, though she'd been a prisoner longer than I'd been alive, still had a youthful appearance. Her hair hung down to her thighs—Maurice never allowed it to be cut—and her eyes were a soft brown, wise beyond her years.

Her hand against mine gave her the ability to read me and speak into my mind. This was how we planned and plotted and how I learned of the dark world that had been thrust upon me. Edith had somehow retained her goodness even in this place and remained my only source of hope.

Maurice kept her there, though he didn't abuse her the same way he did me. I'd determined that he was a little scared of Edith—for when he touched her, she could see him more clearly than he could see himself. She could speak to him of his childhood, of all the bad he'd done. Touching her forced him to see his true nature, the darkness that lurked within his soul. Edith had a way of peering into the depths of a person's being, exposing their deepest secrets and most hidden shames. It was a power that both terrified and intrigued Maurice, for he knew that in her presence, he could no longer hide from the monster he had become. She held a mirror up to his face, reflecting back the ugliness he tried so desperately to conceal.

And yet, despite the fear she instilled in him, he couldn't bring himself to let her go, not even through death. We were his property, and that's all for which we could ever hope.

Not true, she reminded me telepathically. *We were not born to be property. We were born to live free. There is more to this world than darkness and pain.*

She pushed my own memories to the forefront, all the exploring I'd done with my brother, his beloved face. The way the sun felt on my skin and how I relished diving into a cool lake.

You will have that again, Edith assured me. *We both will.*

I attempted to nod but quickly lost consciousness to the pain.

My eyes shot open in the here and now, and for a moment, I was back in that cell, shaking from the cold and aching from the abuse.

Tears had formed and were rolling down my cheeks uncontrollably as I fought against the demons of my own memories.

Forcing myself to suck in a breath, I sat up and braced against the edge of the bed, my pounding heart slowly returning to normal. It had been a long time since those particular memories had come back to me—the nightmare of losing my brother always took precedence.

Aurelia, I can feel your fear. Do you have need of me?

His voice poured over me like the first fresh air of spring rushing through a dusty attic. It still freaked me out that he seemed to be able to read my emotions at will, but for the moment, I basked in the momentary relief from dark memories.

Emerson hovered there, his presence both intruding and comforting, waiting to see how my emotions would go. The comfort won out, and I laid back down, knowing the sun still burned high in the sky.

I hadn't thought about Edith in so long, and that felt like a betrayal. The guilt gnawed at me, a constant reminder of the debt I owed her. Allowing the memory of her to come to me now, without fully realizing or understanding what I was doing, I permitted Emerson to feel what I felt for the woman who had saved my life. My thoughts opened to him, a floodgate of emotions and recollections, and even though I still refused to speak mind to mind, he became swamped by my memories.

Every secret conversation, every terrifying ordeal we lived through together came rushing back in vivid detail. She had been my sanity in a world gone mad, a beacon of hope amidst the darkness that threatened to consume me. She had kept me alive when I wanted to give up, her unwavering strength and determination pulling me back from the brink of despair. When we'd tried to escape, she had given her life for my own, a sacrifice that haunted me every waking moment. Now, she was gone, and I was living this existence, set on wiping shadowmen from the world before I met her in the next, a mission born of vengeance and a desperate need for redemption.

All of this flooded into Emerson's mind, a tidal wave of grief and guilt that threatened to drown us both. Yet he accepted it without censure, his unfailing strength a steadying presence amidst the chaos. He lent himself to me, a silent support that allowed the memories to close, the wounds to begin to heal. He kept the torrent of emotion back, a dam against the flood that threatened to consume me, and in that moment, I knew I was not alone.

I'm so sorry, came Emerson's voice, thick with emotion. *I had no idea. I understand your need to hunt down every one of these creatures and kill them—I have the same need. She was an incredible woman.*

My heart ached, first from the memory of Edith and then Emerson's kind words. More than his words, I felt his conviction and his empathy. I wanted to scream, I wanted to run, I wanted to punch something. Instead, I curled into a ball and squeezed my eyes shut, willing my living nightmares to dissipate and give me a semblance of peace.

Chapter 6

Watching Aurelia walk away was the hardest thing Emerson had ever done. Every single piece of his being screamed in outrage at watching his mate run from him, but he knew if he didn't let her go now, there would be no recovery for their relationship. He knew this, logically, but it didn't make the doing any easier.

Stubborn, beautiful woman.

He couldn't fault her for her beliefs. Though he didn't know the details, it was plain to see she had survived terrible things in her young life. Since she had confirmed that she'd been converted by a shadowman, his imagination needed no more encouragement to fill in the blanks.

All Emerson could really do was set her free and hope that she came back to him. That didn't mean he meant to play fair—on the contrary, he intended to use every means at his disposal to help her see the truth. As for that truth, it was simple; he was a good man who would always put his mate's wants and needs above his own. In the instant that their eyes met in that dark bar, she had become the single most important thing in his life.

The second most important things were due to arrive in a matter of hours. He would wait for his brother and his brother's new mate before following Aurelia. She could run as far and as fast as she wished, but they were connected now. He could and would find her anywhere.

The first bite of pain that wasn't his own came early in the night. The ache bloomed from the point where neck meets shoulder, but the overwhelming disgust that accompanied it told Emerson exactly what had transpired.

Someone—something—had bit his mate.

Rage erupted hot and burned through him in an instant. Fangs grew, and fingers exploded into claws. He would annihilate the beast who dared touch his woman.

Emerson, came his brother's voice. *What's happened?*

He touched her.

Who?

Shadowman.

Take what strength you need. The offer was instant and heartfelt. Dominic's calm helped to keep the blood rage at bay.

Not here. Arie is fighting a dark one.

Emerson got the impression of snapping teeth and a hiss of breath before Dominic spoke again. *Go to her.*

I can't. And he hated that fact with a burning passion that threatened to consume him. When he thought he couldn't hold himself back a moment more, a sudden elation swept down his spine, and Emerson realized Aurelia had defeated the shadowman. With this knowledge, he was able to retract the razor-sharp claws and gleaming fangs that had emerged in his primal rage, allowing him to think clearly once again. *She has won.*

We only have a few hours more on our flight. We will get her back.

I'll see you soon.

Emerson closed his eyes and focused on taking slow, deep breaths in an attempt to quell the tempest of anger and fear that still raged within him. The turbulent emotions demanded release, screamed for an outlet, but he knew that charging into town halfcocked and spoiling for a fight would be reckless and stupid. Not only would it put the innocent human population at risk, but even if he managed to track down one of the shadowmen, engaging in battle now could leave him weakened or injured. He couldn't afford to be compromised, not when Aurelia's very life might depend on him being at full strength to assist her. Emerson clenched his fists, feeling his nails dig into his palms as he struggled to rein in his desperation to act. For Arie's sake, he had to maintain control and stay focused on their mission. Every ounce of his power needed to be conserved for that crucial moment.

When he'd calmed enough to reach out to her, he did so with a light touch. She'd done the work of incinerating the shadowman, but her wound had yet to close. He felt the moment she reached out to the earth, plunged her hands into the rich soil. Emerson had no doubt her connection went beyond the norm for Elementals; the earth would send her the necessary healing herbs. Even when these helped stop the flow of blood, Aurelia stood and staggered, and Emerson could no longer hold back.

Aurelia, you have pushed yourself too hard. Allow me to come to you. He waited with bated breath, but he felt her stubbornness rear its head. *I'm only a call away.*

He didn't fully leave her. He couldn't. Watching as a fly on a wall, he found himself in awe of her. Even with her lagging strength, she healed the earth and made sure there was no sign of the shadowman's presence left in this world. It took what energy she had left, and she sank to the ground.

Emerson waited with her, giving her what he could without being noticed. When he was about to do something about his concern that she wouldn't get to the inn before dawn, she stood and made the trek back. She had to replenish what she'd lost. He waited for her to stop, to feed, but she went to her room and laid down instead. He couldn't hold back any longer. *I can feel your exhaustion beating at me. Why don't you feed?* Again, she didn't answer. He had to keep reminding himself to keep a light touch. *I am here if you have need of me.*

Only when he felt her slip into unconsciousness did Emerson leave his room and head to the airport. He never fully left Aurelia's mind; he couldn't bring himself to be apart from her.

While he stood in the lobby waiting for his brother, Emerson did a routine scan of the humans as they passed. He kept his touch feather-light, his purpose not to be intrusive. He was constantly in information-gathering mode; if any of these humans had been touched by a shadowman, a simple psychic probe would tell him.

Dominic appeared, a heavy duffel slung over one broad shoulder and a slender woman tucked protectively under the other. His first impression of his brother's mate was an attractive, petite woman whose complexion looked paler than was healthy. Despite knowing it was a breach of privacy, he found himself instinctively reaching out with his mind to probe the surface of Reese's thoughts. The impressions that came across were an amalgamation of unease, anticipation, hunger, and nausea.

As if sensing his intrusion, Reese's eyes snapped up to meet his, and Emerson was struck by the fierce intelligence that blazed within their depths. But there was something more, an enigmatic quality he couldn't quite define, a hidden strength that belied her fragile appearance. In that instant, he understood why his brother had been so irrevocably drawn to this woman, and a flicker of grudging respect kindled within him.

The brothers embraced before Emerson turned to Reese. She offered him a bright smile and stuck her hand out to shake; Emerson pulled her in for a hug instead. When he pulled back to arm's length, he kept his hands on her shoulders while he gave her a once-over. "How are you feeling?"

"Well…" she said, reaching out for Dominic's hand. "We have some news."

Concern instantly marring his features, Emerson looked to his brother and spoke privately. *What did the healer say?*

"No need for that," Reese said. "The healer checked me out, and I'm perfectly healthy."

"Forgive me, but you don't look perfectly healthy."

"I can see you're as much a sweet talker as your brother."

"Oh, no, I didn't mean—"

Reese grinned again and stepped closer to Dominic to wrap an arm around his waist. "Should I put him out of his misery?"

"I don't mind if you want to keep messing with him. It's good for him."

She looked back at Emerson, that sparkle in her eye only growing. "We're pregnant."

"Pregnant."

"Yes. Twins, though I suppose that's not a shocker."

"Twins."

"Is he just going to keep repeating everything I say?" Reese asked Dominic.

"I think you shocked him."

"Now you know what you looked like when you heard the news."

Emerson finally blinked. "I'm going to be an uncle?"

"You sure are," Reese said, chuckling as he embraced her once more.

Emerson grinned, then looked back at his brother. Through their bond, he could sense the whirlwind of emotions swirling through Dominic, and there was too much worry mixed in for such happy news. "Wait, how far along are you?"

Reese's smile faded. "About two and a half weeks."

"That means...."

Dominic nodded. "They went through the conversion with Reese. The healer believes that's why she already has morning sickness, but she assured us the girls are healthy."

"Girls?"

"He's doing it again," Reese said, a hint of a smile returning. "We have more to catch you up on, but is there somewhere to eat? I'm starving."

"There's a café a few minutes away."

"Sounds perfect. And then I want to hear all about your mate."

∞ ∞ ∞

EMERSON FOUND HIMSELF TRULY ENJOYING Reese's company as they sat in the cozy café. After she ate her fill, polishing off a hearty bowl of stew and a side of crisp fries, she zeroed in on him with an intensity usually reserved for interrogation rooms. She started asking what seemed like an endless number of questions, eyes sparkling with interest. She wanted a detailed account of every moment since he'd first laid eyes on Arie—what he'd thought, how he'd felt, and what had transpired between them. She seemed especially interested in the spells she'd used to hold him to the bed and block telepathy between him and Dominic.

Reese listened intently as Emerson recounted every moment of their meeting and the undeniable connection they'd shared. When he finished, Reese leaned forward, elbows resting on the table. "What's the plan, then? Where is she right now?"

"She went north and stopped at a village near Ukraine."

"So, when do we leave?"

Emerson paused before answering. "I told her I'd give her space."

"And if she needs our help?"

"You mean Emerson and me, right?" Dominic said. "Because you will stay far, far away from any danger."

Reese pointed at him with her thumb. "Overprotective."

"As he should be. What you carry is too precious to risk."

"Great, there are two of you. Either way, we still need to be close in case she needs the *two of you* to help. It seems like she seeks out danger—not that I blame her—and she seems like a total badass, but even badasses can be outnumbered."

"Agreed, but on one condition." Reese gestured for him to continue, so Emerson said, "We rent a vehicle to drive in. We need to blend, and neither of us wants you to overdo anything."

"Sounds like a perfectly reasonable compromise. Good thing we didn't go far from the airport."

Emerson convinced the two of them to stay in the café while he procured a suitable vehicle for their journey. After careful consideration, he selected a spacious van that would allow Reese ample room to stretch out and relax should the need arise. The van's interior was comfortable and well-maintained, something that wasn't always a given in rural places of Europe.

By the time they set off on their trek, the sun had already passed its apex, casting long shadows across the landscape. Emerson took the wheel, guiding them smoothly along the winding roads, while Reese made herself comfortable in the back. Despite her position, Reese's lively spirit couldn't be contained, and she eagerly led the conversation, the warmth and enthusiasm in her voice catching as they embarked on this unexpected adventure. "What is Arie doing now?"

"Sleeping. She needs to heal."

"Have you spoken to her?"

"There were a couple of times last night I couldn't help myself."

"Did she respond?"

"No."

"You reached out when she needed help, right? Have you tried just having a normal conversation?"

"What do you mean?"

"Like, talk to her. Tell her about yourself. It'll be more of a monologue if she doesn't respond, but it might be the best way to show her who you really are."

Emerson glanced at Dominic, but all his brother did was shrug. "It's worth a shot."

Though the topic changed, Emerson thought about what Reese had said. He needed to get Aurelia to trust him; that was the first and biggest hurdle. Opening up to her might be the only way to do that.

As the sun began its final descent, Emerson stopped for fuel and found a restaurant for dinner. They would continue driving through the night since they had no real need for rest. Since petrol stations weren't always open twenty-four hours like in the States, Emerson made sure to purchase and fill a few gas cans for backup. The van had a rack attached to the back for exactly this purpose, and he took full advantage.

Dominic offered to drive the next leg of their journey, and Reese insisted that Emerson retire to the back of the van to focus his attention solely on Arie. As the last rays of the sunlight faded into the horizon and darkness enveloped the world, a sudden jolt of terror coursed through Emerson's veins. Whatever had caused the spike of fear had woken Arie; he could sense her anxiety and confusion, the disorientation that came with emerging from the depths of slumber into full consciousness. Everything inside Emerson yearned to be at her side, to offer comfort and reassurance, but all he could do was remind her that he was there if she needed him.

Aurelia? Are you all right?

She didn't respond, but her pulse calmed. She wasn't in danger, then. Emerson waited on the periphery, feeling her hunger beating at her. She finally ate and then found four men to drink her fill. A strange, unwelcome feeling came over Emerson when she stepped close to the first male. Her body brushed against his, and Emerson felt his fingers tighten into fists. She sank her teeth into his wrist, and a red haze settled over his vision.

The only thing that stopped him from leaping out of the van to find these men and rip their heads off was Aurelia's utter detachment from what she was doing. She found taking blood to be utterly distasteful, and she saw the men as nothing more than a means to an end. Guilt for taking from them had her leaving money in their pockets, which Emerson found oddly charming.

She left then and continued running through the night. By the time Dominic pulled into the village where Aurelia had spent the last two days, she had found another inn in another small village.

A woman greeted Dominic, Emerson, and Reese warmly before offering a room and breakfast. Emerson requested one room in particular while Dominic and Reese settled into a double for the day.

When he stepped across the threshold, he could feel the remnants of magic in the air. She'd set protections around the room, and he thought she'd left a bit of it intact to protect the inn and its owner.

He could also still make out her scent, and it had the effect of both calming and exciting him.

At the knock on the door, Emerson thanked Cristina for the tray of food before settling in for the day. Whenever Reese was ready to go, they would be on their way.

Taking her advice, Emerson reached out to Aurelia. *Good evening*, he sent to her, feeling ridiculous when she didn't respond. Still, he pushed on. *My brother and his mate have joined me. They were delayed because Reese wasn't feeling well, and they were concerned her conversion hadn't gone well. It turns out that she's expecting. The babies went through the conversion with her. Though they're trying to hide it, I can see how worried they both are. This is not something any of us have heard of before.*

He felt Aurelia's warring emotions, but she didn't ask him to stop. He told her more about Reese and the silly tour she wanted to go on. When he felt Aurelia's amusement, he knew this had been the right call, but he didn't want to push his luck.

I know you asked for space, and I am giving that to you, but I'd like to keep in contact. I think we'll both fare better that way. If you want me to stop, just say so. She remained silent, and Emerson took that as her answer. *Goodnight then, Aurelia.*

As before, Emerson stayed with her, his touch light as air. She didn't sleep, but her breath remained deep and even. It finally seemed as if she were at peace.

And then the first twinge of agony slipped through. Fear, anger, pain. So much pain. Emerson tried to reach her, but whatever held Aurelia in its grip was stronger than their connection. He could do nothing but ride it out with her.

When consciousness finally won, tears streamed down both of their cheeks, though Emerson had no idea why. *Aurelia, I can feel your fear. Do you have need of me?*

She slowly relaxed, but he felt her overwhelming grief take hold, and before either of them knew what was happening, she opened herself up to him, and they were both plunged into her memories. Emerson rode through the storm with her, taking it all in and trying to make it manageable for them both. His heart broke as he lived her past, shattered at the hopelessness of her situation. And the little bit of hope in her dark world—Edith. The same hope that had been ripped away.

I'm so sorry. I had no idea. I understand your need to hunt down every one of these creatures and kill them—I have the same need. She was an incredible woman.

He felt Aurelia latch onto his words even when she still refused to speak. It didn't matter. She had let him in, and that little bit of trust was simply the first domino to be knocked down.

Time would see to the rest. And time was the one thing he had to give.

Chapter 7

A week passed, and then another, the passage of time marked only by the rising and setting of the sun. The days began blending together, one indistinguishable from the next, broken up only by the occasional fight with a shadowman that had the bad luck to cross my path. Emerson's continuous whispers, an unexpected soothing balm to my weary soul, came when the sun reached its apex in the sky, and I was forced to lay inside.

I'd never once responded, and he took that as permission to continue to speak. In truth, I'd come to expect his daily chats—one-sided though they may be. A few days following the onslaught of the memories of Edith, he shared tales of his past, admissions I never could have imagined.

Elementals are tied to the earth, as well as the other elements. It is where our name comes from. You have a deep connection to the earth, more so than I've seen with other Elementals. It's as if she has accepted you as her daughter.

He stayed quiet for a while, and though I refused to respond, I still enjoyed listening to the sound of his voice.

My parents taught Dominic and me about our history. They acted human, though—and in the end, it's what killed them. Dominic and I both learned the old language, which is mostly unknown in our world nowadays. Once, all the Elementals were connected, regardless of race or location. We had a common language and powerful symbols that have long been forgotten.

Dominic met others like us when he was in Minnesota. Though he won't admit it, meeting them gave him hope for the future.

Emerson stopped speaking then, and I thought over what I had learned. The ancient Elemental tongue and symbols Emerson mentioned captivated me most; they might be the crucial weapon to vanquish the shadowmen, specifically Maurice. In my time with Maurice, he never once alluded to anything of the sort, which led me to believe he was equally oblivious to their existence.

It made me wonder how long Emerson's parents had been on this earth. Were they ancient and, therefore, around when the language was used? Or were they part of a legacy of families who passed down the knowledge from generation to generation?

Though I didn't sleep most days, I remained inside and out of the sun. Curling up on one hard bed after another had become an old habit, but I also found myself getting antsy when I didn't hear from Emerson at the usual time. Then he would speak, and everything inside me would settle. Even once he'd bid me good morning—his little joke—the shadow of Emerson's voice kept me company. His soft whispers were becoming the highlight of my day, and I was terrified of what that meant. What would happen if I ever responded.

As the days went on, he continued to speak of what he'd seen of the world and his dreams of the future. Often, he spoke of Elementals and how they were nothing for me to fear. Most often, he told me stories of his childhood.

Our mother loved to throw neighborhood barbecues, he said one bright afternoon. Practically the whole town would show up whenever she was cooking. Dominic and I were nearly inseparable and something of troublemakers—I suppose, like most young boys.

Except we had special abilities that human boys did not. We were unable to shift until our later teens, but we had a good handle on basic element manipulation from a young age. Whenever my mother threw her parties, we liked to play pranks.

There was one time a neighbor was starting up the grill, and we kept it from lighting. When the man bent closer to inspect the coals, we let the fire rise up, and it singed his eyebrows straight off.

How dangerous that was, and yet we were lost to fits of giggles. It took weeks for the hair to grow back. Our father would scold us, and our mother would agree. But then, late at night, she would come into our room and kiss us on our foreheads, and we knew all was forgiven.

He was quiet for a time, and I could sense his melancholy.

I haven't thought of that in quite some time, he admitted. *I hope one day you will be able to meet my brother.*

He still didn't understand that I wasn't running from them or even from him—I was keeping *myself* away, knowing the danger I posed. Knowing I could never be a part of their world.

I remained curled up on the bed, my mind drifting in the silence that remained when Emerson finished speaking. His stories stirred something deep within me—a longing for the life he described, for the family and love that seemed to come so easily to him.

These were not thoughts I could dwell on. They were dangerous, a temptation that could lead me down a path that I couldn't follow. I had to stay focused on my mission—keeping the world safe from shadowmen...and me.

That day, I rested somewhere in Russia, near St. Petersburg—or perhaps that had been days ago. It became increasingly difficult to keep track.

Most nights, I continued to run with no destination in mine, senses attuned to the shadows that lurked just beyond the periphery of my vision. I would stop to rest only when the sun made its appearance, when dawn painted the sky in shades of gold and amber.

There were some cities I would linger for days, even a week, drawn by the unmistakable presence of shadowmen. Under the cloak of darkness, I hunted their ilk, stalking my prey through darkened alleys and deserted wilderness. When daylight broke, I would retreat to whatever temporary sanctuary I'd found, allowing my body to heal and my mind to rest.

But always, the hunt would resume when night fell once more. I was relentless in my pursuit, driven by a sense of purpose that bordered on obsession. I would not stop until the last of the shadowmen had bene expelled from the area, their dark taint wiped clean from the earth. Only then would I move on, seeking out the next city, the next battle in an endless war against the forces of darkness.

This couldn't last forever. I had stashes of money and weapons in various countries, but it would run dry eventually. I'd have to find somewhere to stay for a few months or more, and soon. Laying on a small cot in a hostel, I waited for the sun to begin its descent, thinking out my next move. If I began heading east, I could gather one of my largest stashes in a couple of days' time. It seemed like the best plan for now.

Good evening, came the voice, right on schedule. I settled in to listen. *My brother's mate has been running us ragged. She has an endless amount of energy and a joyful spirit. Dominic is protective, but she doesn't let that stop her.*

I smiled lightly, hearing the equal amount of respect and frustration in his voice. He cared for this woman, Reese. From how he described her, I couldn't help but think I would like her energetic spirit as well.

She is new to this life but sops up knowledge like a sponge. With her pregnancy, her power has tripled what it should be in her learning stage.

It's a lot to manage, but she's doing well. There was a long pause before Emerson said his final words for the day. *I hope you will learn to trust me someday. I am a very patient man, and I will wait for you.*

This made my heart stutter in my chest, a confusing mix of trepidation and exhilaration coursing through my veins. I couldn't quite discern if the sensation was from fear or a growing sense of anticipation. Emerson's presence, his words, and his very essence were gradually infiltrating through my defenses, burrowing deep beneath my skin and taking root in my soul. Despite my best efforts to resist, I found myself increasingly drawn to him, as if an invisible force was pulling me inexorably into his orbit. How long could I withstand his magnetic pull, to fight against the undeniable attraction that seemed to grow stronger with each passing moment spent in his company?

As the sun sank into the horizon, I stood and dressed quickly, wrapping my weapons belt around my hips. My goal was to reach the complete opposite side of the country—which was covered with mountainous terrain and countless enemies, including more shadowmen. They were a plague on this earth and needed to be eradicated. I smiled grimly, prepared for that exact task.

I ran through the night, my mind constantly circling back to Emerson and our daily one-sided chats. The sound of his voice alone had the ability to seep through my skin, pushing back the darkness, if only for a little while. The jumpy nerves and low ache I constantly felt in my body and soul—thanks to Maurice's attentions and conversion—seemed to settle at the mere contact of our minds.

His obvious affection for his brother and Reese had somehow transferred to me, warming my heart even from a distance. And though I'd never met the pair in person, never seen their faces or heard their voices, I felt an unshakable bond with them, as if they were my own flesh and blood. The love Emerson held for them radiated through our connection, igniting a fierce protectiveness within me. I knew without a doubt that I would do anything to keep them safe, to shield them and the precious babies they'd created from any harm that might come their way.

Startled at the thought, I slowed and pressed a palm to my rapidly beating heart. Some unnamed emotion rose up swiftly and silently, nearly choking me with its potency. Did I care for Emerson? Had I forgotten what it was to feel for another human being? No, not a human. But not a shadowman, either. An Elemental.

I still refused to recognize the notion of mates, but what would it hurt to say something back? We could speak telepathically, with a country between us. He wouldn't be in harm's way, and I wouldn't be so damned lonely.

My decision was made. Today, once I found shelter, I would respond to Emerson.

Nerves rumbled in my stomach at the prospect. I didn't have to go through with it. But oh, what a lovely thought. A luxury I'd not permitted myself in the years since I'd escaped Maurice.

As the sun began to rise, I slowed in search of a town. The area was beautiful but remote, and I spotted a cabin nestled in the woods, far from any neighbors or prying eyes. I scanned the area with my eyes and other senses and determined it was abandoned. A few days' rest before I continued with my journey. A serene, safe place to speak to Emerson for the first time.

Approaching the cabin with caution, I found the door unlocked and slipped inside. There wasn't much worry for intruders in so isolated a place. Inside, a thick layer of dust coated every surface. Cobwebs hung from the ceiling like ghostly curtains. But it had a roof and four walls and a well with a pump for water just outside the door. I had made do with worse.

Opening the windows, I stood in the center of the room and gathered energy from the air, winding a spell that cleared the dust and webs. A fresh, light breeze swirled through the space, doing away with the musty smell of neglect.

That done, I lay on the bare mattress and waited for Emerson's voice to fill my mind, steeling my resolve to answer him. Even without his voice in my head, my thoughts were filled with him. What had he done to me? Had he wound some kind of spell? Would I have recognized it if he had?

Curling into a ball, I hugged my knees and mourned the ache in my chest. I couldn't shake the fear that gripped me, the certainty that even if he was a good man and not the evil creatures I hunted, that I would only bring pain and destruction into his life.

Even if he was good, I was not.

Answering him was a terrible idea. What had I been thinking? I would stay in the quiet cabin and simply allow the crushing loneliness to smother me.

I'd been so distracted by my thoughts of Emerson that I didn't notice the way the forest outside had hushed. The hills were silent, not even the smallest animal scurrying in the underbrush. Leaping to my feet, I went instantly on guard. Stepping into the predawn morning, I scanned the area as an eerie sensation crept over me, causing shivers to race down my back and goosebumps to prickle across my skin. I froze on the doorstep, searching the shadowy depths of the forest for any hint of movement or presence.

Yet beyond the ominous feeling that gripped me, I could discern no concrete evidence of malevolence or anything else lurking amongst the trees. That complete absence of sound, more than any noise he could make, was what gave him away.

Knives were instantly in my hands as I realized I'd been tracked, his evil stench in my blood and very soul calling him to me. Maurice.

Flicking the knives into a defensive position, I silently reprimanded myself even as I braced for whatever attack he had planned. Getting upset with myself wouldn't do me any good now. The only advantage I had was that he wanted me alive. I didn't share his sentiment.

Shadows began descending upon me, all too reticent of the first day I'd been taken. My heart pounded out one heavy beat after another, suddenly that scared and innocent twenty-year-old girl again. An echoing laugh beat against my skull, grating against my nerves. Doing my best to ignore his taunting, I called out to the monster that hid in the shadows. "Show yourself, Maurice. Fight me like the man you think you are."

His form shimmered into view, and I didn't hesitate. Whipping out both blades in succession, I immediately followed the sharp steel with my fists, hoping to catch him mid-shift.

I should have known better. Before I could make it two steps, a huge metal net descended upon me, sparking with electricity. Shocks surged through my limbs, rendering me completely useless.

His mocking grin expanded as he sauntered toward my quivering form, wracked by the relentless surges of electricity. With a mere flick of his wrist, he effortlessly halted the trajectory of my airborne daggers, forcing me to observe helplessly through unblinking, widened eyes.

His eyes, a shock blue color that was impossible to forget, watched as I twitched uncontrollably. If his face had been handsome at one time, its appeal had been lost along with the souls he'd corrupted. I could see through the thin façade he presented to the world, to the veiny skin and stained teeth, the bloodshot eyes and stringy brown hair.

When he spoke, his voice produced a shudder that had nothing to do with the volts of electricity flowing through me. I would have given anything at that moment to wipe the smugness off his face. "Hello, pet."

Before I could respond, my body shook violently once more, and darkness descended. The last thing I heard was Emerson's voice inside my head, screaming my name.

Chapter 8

Consciousness crept back gradually as I stirred, senses sharpening one by one. With dawning horror, the gravity of my situation crashed over me like a frigid wave. Every fiber of my being throbbed with a deep, pervasive ache that seemed to radiate from my very core. The unyielding bite of metal shackles encircled my wrists and ankles, their chill seeping into my bones. But worse than the physical bonds was the insidious tingle of dark magic, an invisible snare that sought to suppress my innate abilities.

I inhaled deeply, instantly regretting it as the dank, musty odor of the concrete cell filled my nostrils. Beneath it lurked a more insidious scent—the acrid, sulfurous stench that always accompanied the vile shadowmen. The stale air tasted of despair and suffering, and I fought the urge to gag. Blinking rapidly to clear my vision, I took stock of my grim surroundings, steeling myself for whatever fresh hell awaited me.

"Hello, pet," came the unmistakable voice that sent dread spreading through my limbs. "Welcome home."

Forcing my lashes open, I realized even my eyelids hurt. Whatever that net had been charged with had really done a number on me. "This is not my home," I spat, using all my strength to appear in control. "You're a psychopath if you believe I'd ever stay with you willingly."

Maurice approached, his footsteps echoing ominously in the dimly lit chamber. He reached through the cold metal bars, his fingers roughly gripping my chin and forcing me to meet his icy gaze. His fingers dug into my flesh, squeezing with a cruel intensity until I could feel my skin starting to throb and bruise under the unrelenting pressure.

Despite the barely contained rage simmering beneath the surface, Maurice's tone remained unnervingly steady, his voice a chilling contrast to the fury evident in the ticking of his clenched jaw. His eyes bored into mine with a possessive annoyance, as if my defiance was nothing more than a petulant child's tantrum to be quelled. "I see you still have that sassy mouth. I will enjoy reminding you who it is you obey."

Smirking, he released me and walked away. Struggling against the heavy chains that bound my wrists, I attempted to cry out in frustration at my dilemma but found Maurice had cruelly cut off my vocal cords, rendering me mute. There were several complex layers of magic holding me in place, a tangled web of enchantments that I knew could unravel if only I had use of my hands or voice.

But even worse, I was cut off from Mother Earth, my source of strength and power. Surrounded by thick concrete walls and a hard, cold floor, I felt more alone and helpless than ever before. Hot tears leaked down my cheeks as the full weight and hopelessness of my situation finally sank in. I'd sworn to myself that I would never be held captive again—not by Maurice or anyone else. I silently vowed that I would find a way to escape this nightmare or die trying. There were no other options for me, no other path forward. I had to be strong, had to persevere, for giving up simply wasn't in my nature.

Hours dragged on as I remained trapped and alone, helpless to do anything but contemplate my hopeless situation. Emerson might have come to help me if I'd been able to call out to him telepathically, but Maurice had used the same spell against me that I had against Emerson, sealed by something stronger than his blood. The more I tried to work it out, the more sluggish my mind became, as if a thick fog had settled over my thoughts and made it impossible to think clearly. It seemed Maurice had learned something new in our time apart, as well.

I stopped struggling to undo the spell, realizing my efforts were futile and only draining what little energy I had left. Instead, I allowed my body and mind much-needed rest, knowing that if I got even the slightest fighting chance to escape, I would need a clear head to do so. I focused on my breathing, trying to calm my racing heart and quiet my troubled thoughts.

I'd completely lost track of time, the minutes and hours blurring together in an endless stretch of silence and darkness when I sensed another presence, though I could tell it wasn't Maurice. The sound of heavy footsteps echoed through the room, followed by the clanging of metal and the noxious laughter of one of Maurice's henchmen. The noise was jarring, breaking the oppressive stillness that had settled over the space. But just as quickly as it had come, the disturbance faded away, and the room fell once more into an eerie, unsettling silence.

"Privet?" came a small, frightened voice speaking Russian. "Is anyone out there?"

Another woman. And though I struggled to answer, I still hadn't worked out the spell cutting off my vocal cords. Instead, I clicked the metal cuffs around my wrists together to let the woman know she wasn't alone. Of course, without the ability to speak or let her know I was friendly, the woman gasped in fear and dropped into silent suffering.

Dejected, my shoulders slumped as the harsh reality sank in— my only option now was to wait and continue to work on the spells. I blinked hard, my vision blurring and sharpening in intervals as I tried to decipher the intricate spell holding me captive. Despite the daunting task, I clung to the hope that when Maurice finally deigned to restore my voice, I would be ready to break free from this horrid place. Determination burned within me, fueling my efforts to unravel the complex weave of magic, even as exhaustion threatened to overwhelm my mind and body.

It soon became too difficult to concentrate, though, and so the minutes turned to hours more as I waited and watched, struggling against fogginess and fatigue. Sometimes, I would hear a shuffle from nearby, and I knew the other woman tried to move around, probably terrified and cramped in the tiny space, muscles aching from the prolonged confinement. I wondered who she was, if she was a brand-new addition to Maurice's sick little family, dragged here against her will like I had been, or if she'd been around awhile, trapped in this nightmare for far longer than I could imagine. Did she have a family out there, searching for her? Or was she all alone in the world, with no one to even notice her absence? Was she still human, or had he already corrupted her soul?

The thoughts swirled in my head as I sat there in the darkness, silence broken only by the occasional muffled sob or whimper from my unseen companion. My heart went out to the stranger, and I vowed to do everything in my power to free her.

And myself.

∞ ∞ ∞

WHEN MAURICE RETURNED, I'D MANAGED to focus long enough to come up with the semblance of a plan. It wasn't foolproof by any means, and I still hadn't figured out the specifics of the spell he'd used to trap me here, but it was a glimmer of hope in the oppressive darkness.

I knew I had to act fast before he could enact whatever nefarious scheme he had in mind for me and the other trapped woman. Tensing in anticipation, I prepared to seize any opportunity that presented itself. I wouldn't go down without a fight.

"Hello, pet," he greeted me, reaching through the bars to stroke my cheek.

I cringed back, pressing myself against the cold, unyielding bars, but there was nowhere to go, no escape from his loathsome touch. Every fiber of my being revolted at his proximity, and I'd have spit in his smug, leering face if I thought it would make any difference. Instead, I fixed him with a glare filled with all the loathing and hatred I could muster.

As he methodically undid his handiwork, I watched intently, memorizing the process. The moment the gate opened, he reached in with cruel, grasping hands and hauled me roughly to my feet. I struggled instinctively, but he merely laughed and pulled me hard against him, trapping me against the length of his body in a grotesque parody of an embrace.

"I've missed you, darling," he said, his putrid breath caressing my ear. With one hand, he tugged at my wrist, forcing my palm to cup his manhood. "You see? You see what you do to me?"

Revulsion coursed through me as I tried to wrench my head away, but his fist tightened in my long hair and held me in place. The sharp tug sent shockwaves of pain across my scalp, causing tears to brim, but I refused to let them drop. I would not give him the satisfaction of seeing me vulnerable, of knowing he had the power to hurt me.

Using the grip on my hair as leverage, he forced my mouth to his, pressing so hard my lips mashed against my teeth. When I kept my jaw clenched, denying him entry, he growled and forcibly pried my lips apart with his own. A muffled whimper tried to escape, but it was caught somewhere deep in my throat, trapped by fear and desperation. Left with no other options, I resorted to the only defense I had left.

Snapping my teeth together against his lower lip, I had a moment of satisfaction as he lurched away and glared at me, his hand coming up to staunch the flow of blood.

"It seems I haven't left you alone long enough." Maurice sneered, shoved me back into the cage, and replaced the spell. He stood before me panting with rage when suddenly he brightened and stepped away. "Perhaps you would like to meet your new sister."

The metallic clang and uncanny squeal of an opening cage made my heart plummet. An anguished shriek from the other female captive shredded my soul. Maurice dragged her in front of my cage, his grip on her upper arm enough to bruise, the wound from his lip dripping tainted crimson blood down his chest and to the floor. The young woman's light brown hair had been cut short in a pixie style and highlighted her angular face. Her soft blue eyes clasped onto mine, full of fear and silent pleading.

Maurice watched me carefully as he dragged a sharpened nail down the edge of the woman's cheek, leaving a trail of bright, pure blood in its wake. Swallowing back bile, I tried to convey empathy to her with my eyes alone—though I was afraid to give her any hope.

His cold gaze remained locked on mine as Maurice slowly dragged his tongue along the crimson trail of blood, savoring the metallic taste. With a sudden, vicious motion, he sank his razor-sharp teeth deep into the soft flesh of her neck. He drank deeply and greedily, his throat working as he gulped down mouthful after mouthful of her life essence. The woman struggled weakly at first, her limbs flailing in a futile attempt to break free. But as Maurice continued to feed, her movements grew sluggish and uncoordinated until, finally, she went completely limp in his grasp. I watched in horror, knowing that if he didn't stop soon, he would drain her completely, leaving nothing but a lifeless husk behind.

Since I could sense she carried the Gifted gene, I doubted that was his end game—but then again, I dealt with a highly depraved, psychotic creature. Sense and logic hardly mattered.

Fighting against my own chains, a red haze settling over my gaze as I watched him drain the life from this innocent girl, I struggled in vain to break free. The metal links bit into my wrists, but I barely noticed the pain, consumed by the desperate need to stop this horrific act. Maurice finally pulled away, a satisfied smirk on his blood-stained lips, and allowed her to drop to the ground like a discarded rag doll. She collapsed into a boneless puddle at his feet, too weak to even lift her head, her skin ashen and her breathing shallow. I could only pray that he hadn't taken too much, that there was still a chance to save her.

He waved a hand and freed me. The use of my vocal cords was given back as I slammed against the metal bars of my cage. My fists tightened with crushing force. "You bastard!"

Maurice shrugged as if my remark was inconsequential. "You can save her if you wish."

My heart plummeted into the depths of my stomach as the full weight of his implication crashed over me like a tidal wave. I tore my eyes away from Maurice's smug face and let my gaze fall upon the young woman. She clung to consciousness by a thread, her breaths shallow and labored. As her eyes met mine, I saw in them an emotion I knew all too well—the desperate, primal yearning to live, to survive no matter the cost.

A frustrated groan rose up from my chest, morphing into a feral growl as it passed my lips. In a burst of anger, I slapped both palms against the unyielding iron bars, the metal denting and warping beneath the force of my rage. "Fine," I snarled, my voice rough with barely contained fury. "I'll do it. I'll save her. But tell me, you bastard, what is it you want in return for her life?"

"Why, your obedience, pet. Your promise that you won't try to escape me again."

Closing my eyes, I fought an inner battle. Maurice knew that once I made a promise, I would do everything to keep it. If I gave him my word, I could save this woman's life, but I would be giving him mine in return. A battle waged inside my chest, even as I knew my decision. What other choice did I really have? My eyes slipped open as I muttered, "I accept."

"Say the words," Maurice prompted.

"I promise not to try to escape you." With a triumphant smile, Maurice snapped his fingers, and the cage opened, spilling me onto the ground. I instantly lifted the young woman's head into my lap and looked deep into her eyes. "I'm Arie. What's your name?"

"Anya," she breathed, and had it not been for my excellent hearing, I would not have been able to hear her.

"Do you want to live, Anya?" I asked, not willing to make this decision for her.

She watched me carefully, her soft blue eyes searching mine, seeking answers to questions she couldn't voice. Though she looked utterly terrified, her hair matted with blood and her delicate features contorted in pain and confusion, I saw a remarkable strength in her that I immediately respected. She coughed weakly, crimson blood trickling from the corner of her pale lips, staining her porcelain skin. Her long lashes fluttered and drifted over those beautiful blue eyes, like fragile butterfly wings struggling against the pull of an inevitable fate. But even as her consciousness faded, she managed to utter a single word before she succumbed to the blood loss and passed out in my arms. "Yes," she breathed, her voice barely a whisper yet filled with a fierce determination that echoed through my very soul.

Closing my own eyes, I took a deep breath before bringing her wrist to my mouth. Her blood had to be in my system before the conversion would take hold. I feared taking any more from her, as Maurice had nearly sucked her dry, but I took just enough for our blood to mix before biting into my own wrist, placing it against her mouth, and coaxing her to swallow. I hated the life she would be forced into—but she still had a chance to escape.

Unlike me. And, at least she wasn't getting all of Maurice's blood. I was hoping against hope that my watered-down blood wouldn't affect her as greatly as Maurice's had me.

"I promise to look out for you," I whispered softly, knowing full well Maurice could still hear. "I'll do whatever I can to save you."

"Enough," Maurice commanded, pulling me away. He scooped Anya into his arms and placed her back in her cell to go through the conversion alone.

While he was distracted, I murmured quickly under my breath, praying his attention remained wholly on Anya. For the moment, I'd been freed from my chains but knew they would be back—or that Maurice would take me to an even worse fate. I could only imagine the punishment he would dole out after I'd bit him.

Either way, this was my life now. I might as well get used to it.

Maurice returned and pointed imperiously at the cramped cage. With a heavy heart, I dutifully climbed inside, resigning myself to whatever cruel punishment he had in store for my earlier defiance. After he slammed the cage door shut with a resounding clang and reset the binding spell, Maurice murmured the dreaded incantation to magically sever my vocal cords once again, rendering me mute. Then, with a wicked sneer twisting his lips, he said, "I'll be back momentarily, my disobedient little pet. I've missed you terribly, and I know deep down you've missed me too, despite your willful behavior. Not to worry, we will be intimately reunited soon enough."

With that, he turned and walked away, leaving me alone in the darkness of the prison.

My heart ached with the thought of Anya all alone, unconscious though she was. The life that awaited her would be dark and malicious, but at least she would be unaware for the next few days. That gave me time to plan a way for her to escape.

My fate was sealed, but hers didn't need to be. If I could just get her out, she could find Emerson. He would protect her, even if he remained angry with me for what I'd done. I hoped, in time, he would come to understand I did what I had to do.

Concentrating became less arduous, whether due to regained strength or the gradual fading of Maurice's spell, I couldn't be certain. The gossamer strands of magic that Maurice had woven around me began to take shape before my eyes, their once-invisible patterns now shimmering faintly in the air. With renewed determination, I set to work picking apart the spell's delicate threads, unraveling them one by one in a careful dance of magical skill and sheer force of will. Each loosened coil brought me a step closer to freedom.

"You're not alone, Anya," I said aloud, a grim satisfaction in the ability to speak. The quick spell I'd murmured when Maurice had been carrying Anya to her cell had blocked him from cutting off my vocal cords again. "I promise to get you out of this."

Though I knew I could undo all the spells Maurice had used to imprison me, I restrained myself from doing so. I couldn't escape, and right now, neither could Anya. It would be foolish to tip my hand so early.

Every fiber of my being dreaded Maurice's return, knowing what would be in store for me. Torture, abuse, and lying helplessly while he forced himself on me. I lived with the scars of his abuse every day. He was the reason I could never be a true mate to Emerson. He was the reason I felt a relentless ache every minute of the day. He was the reason I was in a constant battle to fight back the darkness threatening to consume me.

But for all the power he had over me, Maurice couldn't take my mind, my thoughts. He managed to use my body, feast on my blood, and corrupt my very soul, but my thoughts were my own.

It was all I had, and so I spent the long hours waiting, replaying every one-sided conversation with Emerson. I knew now that he truly wasn't like these evil creatures; no, he'd become the light to my dark. A breath of fresh air in this dank prison. He deserved so much more than me.

The concept of having a predestined soulmate felt like a fantastical dream that I was too scared to put my faith in. The shadowmen had taken that wondrous thing and twisted it into something ugly and unrecognizable. At this moment, that no longer mattered; none of it did, for my life was about to be ripped away, no longer under my own control. My sole wish was that Emerson would find love and happiness with someone else in the wide world. Though that thought pained me, I clung to the belief—it was the only way of maintaining the tenuous grasp on my sanity in the face of such a bleak future.

To believe that one day, far from here, Emerson could be happy...without me.

I'd been sitting so long in the oppressive darkness and deafening quiet that the abrupt, jumbled sound of pounding footsteps made me flinch. The cramped space flooded with other shadowmen—Maurice's lackeys. They moved with swift precision, seizing Anya from her cell and working at releasing me.

Something unexpected must have occurred, an event that Maurice hadn't anticipated. As one of the shadowmen wrenched open the cage door with a resounding clang, I wondered idly at the possibilities. The shadowman grasped my arm in an unyielding grip, hauling me unceremoniously to my feet. "You're coming with us."

After being confined in that cramped cage for so long, my muscles protested, and I stumbled forward with an unsteady gait. I kept my mouth resolutely shut, feigning the restricted use of my voice that the binding spell had supposedly inflicted upon me, and decided not to make it easy for my brutish captors. My momentary struggles earned me a vicious backhand across the face, the force of the blow knocking me to the hard ground and instantly raising a throbbing bruise on my cheek. Another of the vile creatures gave my aggressor a pained look. "Maurice won't be happy with that."

"She'll heal," he replied with no remorse, gripping my upper arms tightly as he hauled me to my feet. In one swift motion, he slung me over his broad shoulder like a sack of potatoes, paying no heed to my futile attempts to break free. My feet kicked wildly in the air, connecting with nothing but empty space as I struggled against his iron hold, heart pounding with a mixture of fear and indignation at the callous treatment.

Six shadowmen had been sent to collect Anya and me, four of whom were acting as guards. Something serious had definitely happened, and I cursed at the timing. If Anya had at least been awake, this would have been a good time to attempt her escape.

If Maurice was being forced on the run, that meant his security wouldn't be as tight.

The shadowmen carried us through the dank dungeon and up through an equally depressing building before finally bursting into the night. I took a deep breath of the fresh air, instantly feeling my connection to the earth even though I was still being carried like a sack of potatoes. Most of the spells were off me, apart from the bubble preventing telepathic speech, so now I just had to choose my moment.

A thought occurred to me. I promised not to try to escape Maurice, but I never promised not to kill him. Sure, it would take me with him—even if I got the upper hand on Maurice, I would be greatly outnumbered by his lackeys. But Emerson....

If I could release myself from the spell blocking my telepathy, I could let Emerson know where I was and to come save Anya. He would make sure she survived in this new life. With him, she could have a fighting chance.

Maurice came into view, and even from my prone position, I straightened my shoulders on seeing him.

"My apologies, pet. Our reunion will have to be postponed," he said, brushing my hair away from my face. His lips smothered mine, and I did everything in my power to keep my mouth closed, my body rigid. It was awkward, to say the least, since I hung upside down over one of his henchmen's backs. When Maurice pulled away, I prepared for him to beat me for resisting, but when he spotted the bruise high on my cheek, he sucked in an audible breath. "Release her."

The shadowman who carried me did so immediately, knowing the punishment he'd receive. Maurice backhanded him, much as the guard had done to me.

"You dare lay a hand on my mate?" Maurice hissed. "You will pay for that."

Maurice became distracted as he focused on doling out punishment on the shadowman who had dared to harm me. His attention was fully consumed by his rage, and I knew this would be my sole chance to act. In the precious few moments of relative freedom his distraction afforded, I quickly closed my eyes and murmured the words to reverse the spell that had been keeping me from reaching out to Emerson. I felt the magical barrier dissipate, but my hands remained restrained by the unyielding cuffs behind my back. Saving Anya was more important. Freeing my hands would be my next challenge, but for now, at least my telepathic connection to my mate was restored.

As soon as the last dredges of the spell fell away, I could sense Emerson's presence as if he'd been waiting for our connection to return. For the briefest moment in time, I reveled in his warmth and the certainty of our connection that I finally had come to terms with.

Emerson, I breathed in relief before he could speak. *I was captured by a shadowman named Maurice in Russia. He has another woman captive; her name is Anya. You need to find her and save her. It's...it's too late for me.*

Aurelia! I am coming to you now. I won't lose you.

His words warmed my heart, but this would be my only chance to fight. I would lose, but I would no longer be a prisoner. At least Anya had a chance now.

Save Anya, I reiterated to Emerson. As I began reversing the spell that bound my hands, Maurice spun and glared at me, accusation shining in his eyes.

"What have you done!" Before I could move, his fist came down, and I sprawled on the ground, fighting consciousness and groaning in pain. He stalked over to me, his breaths coming in terrible gasps as he stared down at my prone form.

He had murder in his eyes, the red haze as terrifying as his elongated fingers sharpened into claws at the tips. This would be it, then. I struggled to rise, to fight back. To take him with me as I met my end.

Knowing I had limited time, a final thought winged its way across the night.

Emerson, I'm sorry.

Chapter 9

The very air trembled with rage as a storm heralded the arrival of death. Lightning crackled across the sky, illuminating the ominous clouds that swirled above. They descended upon the earth as two avenging angels, their forms cloaked in shadow and fury with deep green eyes glinting with fierce determination. Dark and menacing in their quest, they radiated an aura of power that sent shivers down my spine. I sucked in a breath as the two figures shimmered into view, their outlines becoming clearer with each passing second. My heart skipped a full beat before it began to race, pounding against my chest as I stared, transfixed, at the sight before me. The earth itself seemed to quake beneath their feet, acknowledging the raw energy that emanated from their presence.

Emerson had been close enough to arrive less than a minute after I'd called out to him, his swift appearance both reassuring and unnerving. I tried to calm my racing heart, reminding myself he was there to help me, not harm me. He'd brought his brother along with him, a mirror image of Emerson in every way. They were identical, from their sharp, chiseled jaws to their glittering emerald eyes that seemed to hold the promise of retribution for any who dared to cross them.

Maurice backed away from my sprawled body, his lip pulled back in a snarl as his men closed rank around him. While they prepared for an attack, I continued to work on my restraints. Pushing to my knees, I watched as the wind whipped and lightning streaked across the dark sky. The twins' arrival had been exactly what I'd needed to distract Maurice and complete my task.

Mother Earth, strong and true. Release me from my bonds so I may live to fight another day.

She responded instantly, two mounds of earth covering my feet and caressing up my calf, reaching toward the invisible restraints. Lightning danced across the sky and struck the ground dangerously close to the shadowmen as they crouched for attack.

Emerson locked his fierce gaze on a single shadowman, channeling his mind to unleash a torrent of agonizing pain upon the dark creature. As the shadowman writhed and shrieked, Dominic whirled into action, his tattooed arms a blur as he fought to keep the other menacing entities at bay. He dodged and parried their shadowy claws, determined to protect his twin while Emerson maintained his mental assault. But Emerson's gift had its limits; he could only focus his power on one foe at a time. The remaining shadowmen soon began to overwhelm Dominic, their numbers too great for him to fend off alone.

The shadowman who had been carrying Anya dumped her limp form onto the ground. As the earth loosened the shackles that had been restraining me, I used my newfound freedom to chant, the words flowing from my lips like a river. *Mother Earth, protector of life. Cover Anya, keep her from strife.*

As the earth began to layer in a protective shell over the young woman, I turned my focus wholly onto the ringleader of the shadowmen.

Maurice. My mortal enemy.

Even with my weapons gone, I used what I had—my raw strength and fury. I focused my power, channeling it into a concentrated burst of energy that I aimed directly for the vile creature, determined to put an end to his malevolent reign once and for all.

Knowing my magical assault alone wouldn't be sufficient to defeat him, I followed it up by launching myself toward him with every ounce of speed I possessed. Maurice, however, reacted with lightning-quick reflexes, spinning at the last possible instant. His hands latched onto my shoulders just as my fingers brushed against his neck. Exploiting my forward momentum, he wrenched me off balance, twirling me around in a grotesque parody of a dance. With a brutal twist, he flung me away from him, sending me hurtling through the air like a discarded ragdoll.

Rolling to my feet, I immediately launched at him again, switching up my tactics now that he had turned to face me. I let out a flurry of punches, which he easily blocked. In a lightning-fast move, I extended my leg, sinking into the soft flesh of his stomach.

He stumbled back with an oomph, glaring at me as he regained composure. Still, he couldn't resist taunting me. "Give up, pet. These men will be defeated soon, and you will be mine once again."

"Piss off," I replied, lunging toward him again.

I remained relentless in my attack, forcing Maurice to defend and giving him no time to return the favor. He slowly backed up, nearing a tree and my trap, when I saw something in my peripheral that had me hesitating just a moment too long.

Emerson and Dominic were overwhelmed, both locked in fierce physical combat against the relentless onslaught of shadowmen. Dominic grappled with three of the dark entities, his muscles straining as he fought to break free from their unyielding grasp. A blinding flash of light erupted as a lightning bolt struck one of the shadowmen square in the chest, the crackling energy causing it to convulse and collapse. The remaining two shadowmen faltered momentarily, their shadowy forms flickering with uncertainty, giving Dominic the crucial opening he needed to turn the tide of the battle.

Beside them, Emerson fought with the ferocity of a cornered lion, his movements fluid and precise despite the overwhelming odds. Two shadowmen managed to latch onto his arms, wrapping around his limbs like chains, while a third coiled itself around his neck, attempting to choke the life from him. A fourth shadowman landed before Emerson, its fingers elongating into wickedly sharp claws, poised to tear into the flesh of his chest.

In the split second I had taken to assess the dire situation my companions faced, Maurice seized the opportunity to strike. His hand connected with my cheek in a vicious backhand, the force of the blow landing directly on the pre-existing bruise that marred my skin. The impact sent me flying sideways, my body crumpling into a heap as I hit the ground. Pain exploded through my skull, my vision swimming with hazy spots of light as I struggled to regain my bearings. But even as I lay there, dazed and disoriented, the flames of anger surged within me, fueling my determination to rise once more and renew my attack against our merciless foe.

My trap may not have worked, but I still had Mother Earth on my side.

Glaring at the evil creature who had turned me into one like him, I shoved my hands into the earth, finally able to feel the connection fully. *Mother Earth, strong and true. Hold these vile creatures with your great power. Help us win, though we be but few. Make these creatures kneel and cower.*

Massive, gnarled vines erupted from the earth, coiling around the legs of the few remaining shadowmen like serpents. The thorny tendrils dug into their rotting flesh, immobilizing them where they stood. I maintained my steely focus on Maurice, but in my peripheral vision, I witnessed Emerson crumple to the ground as the shadowmen finally released their hold on him.

A searing pain lanced through my heart at the sight of Emerson's prone form, but I forcefully pushed it aside. Infused with a strength I had never before possessed, I prowled forward with single-minded determination. It wasn't just the raw power of the earth flowing through my veins—somehow, Emerson had transferred his remaining energy to me as well. Rather than wasting precious time questioning his actions, I surged ahead, rapidly closing the distance to my target.

"Goodbye, Maurice," I said through gritted teeth, not giving him a chance to respond.

Pure rage flowed through me, extended my fingers into claws. I shoved my fist through his chest and ripped out his black heart with my bare hands. The same as his lackeys had been attempting to do with Emerson—only I succeeded. His blood stung and burned my skin, but watching the fear in the realization of his defeat skitter across his face made every searing pain worth it. A fireball lit in my palm with a thought, disintegrating the heart before I sent it flaming into the creature's body, finding an odd sort of enjoyment in his agonizing shrieks.

Knowing the earth would keep him secure until he'd burned to ash, I turned and helped Dominic finish off the rest of them. Helpless as they were in the thick vines, it was quick work to send a ball of flame into each. When we finished the distasteful task, I rushed to Emerson's side only to find his face pale and his eyes closed, his temperature dangerously low.

"Emerson," I said sternly, cupping his face with my palms. "You idiot, you will come back to me now."

"His injuries are grave," said the man who looked so much like my mate. "He needs blood and a healer."

My gaze shot up to his in panic. "I can't give him my blood, and there are no healers here."

"He can have mine."

Shaking my head, I took in his state and said, "You can't afford to lose any blood."

"My mate is near," he explained gently. "She will replenish me."

As he spoke, a petite woman with shoulder-length brunette hair and wide, earthy eyes appeared at his side. "Yes, I will," she said, then sent me a little wave. "Hi, I'm Reese."

I found my lips tipping up in a half smile as Dominic knelt beside Emerson's still form, biting into his wrist and placing the wound over his brother's mouth. My hands were pressed against the terrible, ragged wound over Emerson's heart, the adrenaline from the fight slowly leaking from my body and leaving me drained.

"He's not responding," Dominic said with a trace of panic.

Our eyes met, and something in his gaze spurred me into action. Fighting off panic, I made myself think rationally. "We need to find a place away from here."

"We can't move him," Dominic began to argue, but I had already scooped the large man into my arms.

"Join me or don't. I won't lose him now." Without another word, I began to run, forcing my weakened limbs to move. We had to get away from the scene of death and into fresh earth.

This had to work. *You hear me, Emerson? You will survive this because I can't lose you. I'm sorry I ran. We still have a lot to work out, but I'm willing to try. I need you to fight. You hear me? Fight!*

Finding a patch of rich earth, I slowed and laid him carefully among the potent soil. Digging my hands into the earth, I asked another favor. *Mother Earth, strong and true. Accept this man as one of your own. Heal him from his wounds—he is my mate, my home. In your name, I ask this of you.*

I sat back as the earth rumbled and began to move up and around Emerson, enclosing him completely in the soil. Scooting back, I stared at the mound now in front of me, uncertainty suddenly crashing down.

Barely aware of another's presence, I started when Dominic spoke from behind me, his voice hard and angry. "You've killed him."

Standing, I held my ground as I faced off with Emerson's brother. Through my bare feet, I received messages from the earth and needed Dominic to see reason before he did something stupid.

"I'm saving him," I said stubbornly, lifting my chin in defense. "The earth has accepted him and is attending his wounds."

His distrust was plain on his face, but when his mate placed a gentle hand on his forearm, Dominic's face relaxed. "She's right, Dominic. Listen."

They were both attuned to nature, as Emerson had said all Elementals were. I waited, none too patiently, while they came to their own conclusion. Dominic finally nodded once, his arms crossed and his jaw firm. I would take it.

"It's nice to meet you," Reese ventured, staying by Dominic's side.

With a sigh, I relaxed my position and knelt beside the mound. For some reason, I felt the need to explain myself. I didn't care for the sensation. "It's strange for me to trust anyone but myself. But it's nice to meet you, too. I'm Arie."

Reese nodded and smiled, then took a step forward. Dominic restrained her, and I could see something pass privately between them. She turned to me once again. "You'll have to forgive Dominic; he's a little overprotective. Tenfold since we found out I'm pregnant."

My gaze drifted to her flat, toned stomach before meeting her eyes once more. A peculiar yearning stirred deep within me, a longing I couldn't quite define. The earth whispered to me, sending a steady stream of updates about the life growing inside Reese, but even that felt insufficient. I rested my hands gently over the place where Emerson resided, feeling the warmth of his presence beneath my palms. "Congratulations," I said, my voice soft and sincere. "What a beautiful gift you've been given."

"Thank you." Reese shot Dominic a look that plainly said, *I told you so*, and knelt beside me. "What is happening to him?"

"There was a lot of damage. The shadowman tried to claw out his heart. The earth is doing everything to help him, but it will take time." My eyes flicked back over the couple, taking in the exhaustion Dominic did everything in his control to hide. "You need to feed. I will watch over Emerson."

"No, I will stay here."

"I'll go," Reese volunteered.

This was met with a dark look by her mate. "You cannot go alone."

She rolled her eyes at me and let out an exaggerated sigh. "See? Overprotective."

"With good reason." Dominic paused and let out a breath of his own. "Fine, we will feed, and then we will return."

"I'll be here," I said with little humor. Before they could leave, I remembered Anya, and my voice cracked. "Please, on your way back—get Anya. She's going through the conversion, and she should be away from that scene of death."

Dominic searched my gaze for a moment longer before nodding once and dissolving into the form of a bird. Before she followed suit, Reese reached out and squeezed my shoulder. "We'll take care of her."

"Your brother is annoying," I said aloud to Emerson once they'd taken wing, knowing he couldn't hear me but that Dominic probably could. "Must be a family trait."

From far away, a bird squawked, so I knew my gibe had hit home. It gave me grim satisfaction in a terrifying situation. The man lying beneath the earth had burrowed his way into my world, into my heart. I wasn't even sure when it had happened—sometime between him nearly getting killed attempting to save me to his soft whispers, speaking about a world I never even allowed myself to imagine.

Lying beside the mound of earth, I placed a hand over where I believed Emerson's chest would be. Our telepathic link wouldn't work, as the earth must have put him in a catatonic state in order to heal. Instead, I whispered aloud. Words poured from my heart and soul. "You need to survive this. Before you, my life was bleak and hardly worth living. I never expected to live through another confrontation with Maurice, but I did because of you. Now, the only reason I have to live is to see where this relationship goes. For the first time in more years than I can count, I'm optimistic about my future. My future with you.

"You hear me, mate? You will survive this. Because I need you."

Being trapped by Maurice forced me to examine myself and my feelings. I now saw the truth in his claim—we were mates.

And I would do anything to ensure his safety and survival.

Chapter 10

For three long nights, I vigilantly sat beside Emerson's earthen enclosure, my connection to the earth providing me with constant updates on his condition. As the sun rose each day, I fastened a makeshift canopy to shield me from its harsh rays, and when night fell, I lay beside him, gazing up at the twinkling stars that dotted the inky sky.

Dominic and Reese returned with Anya, who had also been embraced by the earth as one of her own. They carefully placed her in a mound next to Emerson, allowing me to keep a watchful eye on both of them as Emerson healed and Anya underwent her transformation. The air was thick with anticipation and hope, and I found myself silently praying to the elements for their swift recovery.

Dominic and Reese were there for the majority of the time, though Dominic's concern for Reese's health meant she slept a few hours each day in an actual bed. They also brought me meals, though I refused to feed from Dominic. It was a habit to go long periods of time without blood, and it wasn't like I expended much energy just sitting around.

Reese and I talked a lot—well, she talked a lot, and I listened. Dominic seemed content to do the same. On the first night, she asked, "Do you have any extra abilities?"

"Not that I know of," I said. "Do you?"

Reese grinned, her eyes lighting with excitement. "I can control electricity."

That was new to me. Of course, most of the powers I'd seen had been corrupted by shadowmen, and it wasn't like we were having conversations about it. Something clicked then, thinking back to the fight with Maurice and the sudden lightning storm. "Does that include lightning?"

"Yup," she answered proudly. "Discovered that by necessity, and it's not exactly something I get a lot of practice with."

Glancing over at Dominic, I said, "I can imagine. What do you mean, you discovered it by necessity?"

Reese shifted closer to Dominic as she explained, "I was captured by a shadowman. He was using me to bait Dominic, and, of course, it worked. They fought, and the shadowman left us to die in a fire. I don't even really remember how I did it, but my anger fueled enough electricity to create a bolt of lightning."

"That was a pretty spectacular hit," I said, referring to the strike that had given Dominic the upper hand in our battle.

"I was trying to do more. Maybe if I had, Emerson wouldn't be...." She trailed off, gesturing toward the mound of earth beside me. Reese obviously took our current situation to heart.

"You saved your mate," I said quietly. "And Emerson will be just fine. He wouldn't want you to blame yourself."

"Your connection to the earth is greater than most Elementals," Dominic pointed out after a moment.

"That's true," Reese said with wide eyes. "Maybe that's your extra gift."

It didn't feel that way to me—more that I listened to her whispers and rhythms. I always strived to give back more than I took, to nurture and respect the land that sustained us. But rather than trying to explain this, I simply shrugged, not wanting to argue the point. "Maybe."

"Dominic can tell when someone's lying," Reese added. He stiffened and gave his mate a mildly annoyed look.

"You can?"

He nodded. "It came in handy when I first met Reese."

Raising an eyebrow toward her, I didn't need to ask for her to answer. "I was working overnights at a retail store under false pretenses. I'm a writer, and I'd come up with a whole backstory of a character.... Needless to say, most of what I said came out as untruthful."

My mouth turned up in a smile. "That's funny."

The loving look that passed between them made me feel like an intruder, and I quickly looked away, my own heart squeezing like a vice.

The following evening, as the sun dipped below the horizon and the stars began to twinkle in the inky sky, I approached Dominic with a question that had been weighing heavily on my mind ever since I first encountered Emerson. The bond between mates was a mystery to me, an enigma that I yearned to unravel. I needed to understand the depth and complexity of this connection, to grasp the intricacies that wove two souls together in an unbreakable thread of destiny. With a determined glint in my eye, I gathered my courage and asked Dominic directly, hoping that his experience could shed light on the perplexing nature of this powerful bond.

"How strong is your psychic connection?" I asked, gesturing between him and Reese.

"We are able to speak telepathically, as all mates are. Reese also seemed to connect to my memories as she slept—she had dreams of my life. Jade, the woman we met recently, told us she had done the same with her mate, Talon. Why do you ask?"

"Emerson...does he...is he able to do more with you, other than speak telepathically?"

Dominic thought this through before responding. "He's always been able to tell when I'm upset or angry, even if we're not nearby. I never thought about it as anything more than our twin connection, but I suppose it might be."

"It's almost as if he can read my mind sometimes," I murmured, staring at the ground. "It's unnerving."

Reese spoke up this time. "I wonder if, because of his ability, he's able to have a stronger connection to both of you."

"What do you mean?" Dominic asked.

"Well, the brain is just another muscle. I imagine having a psychic ability, like being able to harm someone with a thought, takes a lot of exercise. Maybe because of that, he's able to do more than we are."

"Maybe it's something we're all capable of with enough practice." Dominic considered Reese's assertion for a moment. "That's an interesting thought."

"It makes as much sense as anything else I can come up with," I said with a wry smile.

The third night, Reese told me about a threat worse than shadowmen—as if I needed another thing to worry about. She told me how her babies had gone through the conversion with her—though I already knew that from Emerson's daily whispers—which led her to their most recent trip before meeting up with Emerson.

"There's a woman named Reya who is a healer. She examined me the day we flew to Europe to look for Emerson. She told me the babies seem healthy, but we have no idea how the conversion will affect them."

"That is pretty incredible," I agreed.

"The group that we stopped to see—well, they had some trouble with shadowmen and...daemons."

I blinked once, not fully comprehending what she'd just said. "Daemons?"

Reese nodded, her hands resting protectively against her stomach. "Apparently, the daemons have been corrupting Elementals for centuries, turning them into shadowmen. Kate, who I was telling you about, along with Jade, they were able to help the shadowmen. Virtually restore their souls. It's really rather amazing."

My incredulous gaze switched between Reese and Dominic, expecting one of them to tell me she was kidding. Dominic's reserved but serious look told me otherwise. "That can't be true."

"It sounds crazy, I know, but I saw the shadowmen they saved—met them. They'd already saved nearly thirty of them by the time we arrived."

"How could you ever trust such evil creatures?" I asked, finding my anger rising.

"Believe me, I understand how you feel," Dominic said, sensing my emotions about to spill. "My hatred for shadowmen runs deep, as does Emerson's. But...it's true. Not all were able to be saved— the ones who had turned to the darkness on their own, it seems. But the rest—their souls were corrupted, and those women gave them a second chance. Everyone deserves a second chance, don't you think?"

Pressing my lips together into a thin line, I realized any argument I gave would ultimately work against me. We were silent for a while before Reese began to speak again. "I've stayed in contact with Jade since we've been here. The day we left California, they went to search for a friend of hers, who turned out to be Tristan's sister. Lani. She was living in New Mexico, and apparently, the entire town underwent a daemon attack."

"What? How have I not come across such creatures?"

Reese shrugged. "Maybe you have. Jade told me they show their true forms in the three nights of the full moon—horns and all— but they can look like humans otherwise. Really tall humans, but still."

"This all seems rather incredible."

"Four daemons turned against their leader," Reese said, then continued to tell me the whole story. Of Balor, king of daemons, and his connection to the Tuatha Dé Danann. How original Fomorian daemons didn't have a soul, but those with a Tuatha Dé Danann parent did. And how Balor had sent his men out into the world to corrupt Tirog's creations—the Elementals.

Anger rose hot and fast. "Balor created Maurice. It is because of him I have been doomed to this life. We must end him."

Reese's wide eyes looked at Dominic as if she didn't know how to respond to my edict. Dominic reached out to squeeze her hand before answering me. "They are planning to infiltrate the daemon city of Murias on Samhain in order to free sympathetic daemons along with any captives being held. After that's been completed, I have no doubt plans will be put in place to launch an attack."

"Then I shall assist with that." Silence settled between us. I could see the arguments written across both their faces, but in this, I wouldn't be deterred. If I could exact vengeance for my brother's death—for Edith, for me—I wouldn't hesitate in joining that fight. Clearing my throat, I changed the subject to distract them from the topic of daemons. "You need to find a healer. What is your plan once Emerson is released from the earth?"

"There is another healer nearby, but he's dealing with some problems of his own before he can meet with us. Hopefully, he will be here soon, and he can check over Emerson when he's healed, too."

"The earth is doing a good job," I said, instantly defensive. I didn't like the idea of another stranger around, whether or not he was a healer.

"Of course," Reese said, instantly contrite. "I didn't mean that. I'll just feel better when he can examine me."

Nodding, I looked away, unsure what else to say.

"Arie?" Reese asked hesitantly. "When Emerson was first injured, you told Dominic you couldn't give him your blood. Would you tell me why?"

Sighing, I decided to tell her the truth. Somewhere between being captured by Maurice and calling out to Emerson, I'd made the decision to embrace this mate thing. And this was Emerson's family, so they had a right to know what they were getting into.

"Maurice—the shadowman that was leading the ones we fought—he captured me five years ago. I was a human and apparently Gifted. He took my blood and fed me his." I paused here, barely able to get the words out. "I was converted by an evil monster."

Reese immediately sat forward to place a hand on my arm, her eyes filled with sympathy. Dominic sat rigid, his eyes cold and hard, though oddly not directed at me. Part of me thought they should have been.

"My soul is darkened, and his blood runs through my veins. It's poisoned with Maurice's own concoction—his way of making sure I lived every day in misery. It also made it easier for him to track me."

"That's horrible," Reese said softly. "I'm so sorry."

Shrugging, I attempted to keep my voice light. "There is no use in regret. My life is what it is—I fully planned on leaving this world and taking Maurice with me. Now...." My hand ran along the earth, over where Emerson lay immersed. My heart hurt when I thought of how close I'd come to losing him before I'd even had him. "Now, I have a chance to start over."

We fell silent for a long time as we all became lost in our own thoughts again. Reese spoke first. "When Jace arrives, you should allow him to examine you. He might be able to help."

"No one can help me," I replied hoarsely.

Before Reese could argue, the earth began to tremble. Just low murmurs, gradually strengthening into quakes. We all stumbled back, uncertain of what was happening.

With wide, disbelieving eyes, we watched as the earthen mound holding Emerson's body shivered and trembled, chunks of dirt and debris rolling off the edge in a cascading shower of soil. The ground continued to shake and undulate, the movement reminding me of a massive trommel sorting for precious gold nuggets. Emerson emerged from the depths moments later, his form rising from the earth like a phoenix from the ashes, and as he fully surfaced, the earth finally stilled and settled. We all stared at the unmoving man, unsure of what to do next, our hearts pounding with a mixture of fear and anticipation.

His emerald green eyes shot open as he gasped for breath, his chest heaving with the effort of drawing air into his lungs. As if knowing exactly where I stood, his gaze locked on mine. "Arie," he said softly, relief palpable in his tone. "You're all right."

Kneeling beside him, I placed one hand on his arm and the other behind his neck, carefully helping him into a seated position. "Thanks to you. How do you feel?"

"Different, but completely healed," he replied, pressing the heel of his hand against where the wound in his chest had been.

Dominic knelt on his other side, offering his wrist. "Feed, brother."

Accepting the offer gladly, Emerson drank his fill before thanking Dominic. "How long has it been since we encountered the shadowmen?"

"Three days," Dominic said. "Your mate asked the earth to heal you, and she did. It was rather incredible."

The begrudging respect in Dominic's tone caught me off guard. It was a rare occurrence, and for him to express even a hint of admiration was a testament to the extraordinary nature of what had transpired. His gaze, usually sharp and critical, now held a glimmer of acknowledgment, a silent nod to my power and resilience. It filled me with a strange warmth.

"You've been beside me that whole time?" Emerson asked, his eyes back on mine. The infusion of blood had given him color back in his cheeks, and his energy seemed renewed. "Even during the day, when the sun hurts you?"

"Of course," I said, matter of fact. "I am your mate, after all."

His answering smile lit my entire world.

Chapter 11

Dominic gently grasped his brother's arm, supporting him as he rose unsteadily to his feet. Emerson's limbs trembled, the muscles atrophied from his prolonged slumber. I watched from a distance, heart swelling with a mix of joy and trepidation. Though I had spent countless hours by Emerson's bedside, listening to his murmured dreams and secrets, I now felt like a stranger in his wakened presence. The connection I had forged with his unconscious mind seemed fragile and uncertain when faced with the reality of his piercing green eyes and towering form. Shifting my weight awkwardly, I was unsure of my place in this intimate moment between the reunited twins.

Partly because he was so *good*-looking. It sent all my systems into overdrive and my heart racing. I didn't know how to deal with that—was terrified to deal with that.

Moreover, I had grown accustomed to hearing him speak without needing to gaze into his captivating eyes, which now left me feeling vulnerable and exposed. But now, as his eyes locked with mine, a torrent of emotion surged forth, threatening to engulf me in its sheer intensity. Overwhelmed, I sought distraction, making my way to where Anya's form still rested within the earth's embrace—only for the ground to shudder once more beneath my feet, forcing me to retreat. She rose from the soil much like Emerson had, her lithe frame emerging as if born anew. There she lay, eyes closed, oblivious to our collective stares, a picture of serenity amidst the chaos.

Anya jolted into consciousness, her eyes flying wide as a sharp intake of breath escaped her lips. Using my speed to be at her side, I placed one hand on her arm as I spoke as soothingly as possible. "Shh, it's all right. You're safe now," I assured her in Russian.

"What...what's happened?" she asked, obviously bewildered by not only all the events that had happened to her but to be waking up in a forest surrounded by strangers.

"It's a long story. Let's get you somewhere more comfortable first, and I'll explain everything."

Reese ventured closer, her footsteps nearly silent on the forest floor. She crouched down beside Anya, her movements graceful and fluid, as I gently helped the disoriented woman into a sitting position. Anya's eyes darted between us, confusion and fear evident in her soft blue gaze.

To my surprise, Reese began speaking to Anya in Russian, her words flowing smoothly and naturally. Her voice was soft and soothing, a stark contrast to the tension that hung in the air around us. I couldn't help but be impressed by Reese's linguistic abilities. I supposed that was one of the many benefits of being an Elemental—

the ability to retain vast amounts of knowledge, including multiple languages, with ease. "Hi, I'm Reese. You're safe with us. Do you have family near here?"

Anya's head swayed from side to side as glistening droplets welled up in her soft blue eyes, clinging to her lower lashes like morning dew on a delicate petal. I sensed there was an extensive tale behind her reaction, a story of pain and heartache that had left deep scars on her soul, but now wasn't the time for such a conversation. Glancing at our modest assembly—Reese, Dominic, Emerson, and myself—I arrived at a decision. Uttering a whispered incantation to induce slumber, ancient words of power that flowed from my lips like a gentle breeze, I delicately pressed my fingertips against Anya's temples, feeling the warmth of her skin beneath my touch. As the spell took hold, I supported her weight, cradling her petite frame in my arms as she drifted off into oblivion, her breathing slowing to a steady rhythm and her features relaxing into a peaceful repose.

"Dominic? Can you carry Anya?" I asked, knowing he was the only one of us at physical peak.

"Of course," he said, approaching with caution. Once Anya was secure in his arms, I stood and faced Emerson.

"So, what now?" Reese asked brightly, ready to be on our way.

Emerson and I were locked in a gaze, barely aware of the world around us. Dominic cleared his throat in an attempt to break the tension, but it did no good. "We have rooms at an inn not far from here. You both need to regain your strength before we make any decisions."

Emerson nodded as he drew near me with measured steps. "You will stay with me?" *Please?*

How could I refuse his pleading look? Not trusting my voice, I simply nodded and began to move away. Kneeling beside the opened mounds of earth, I dug my hands into the ground and uttered a few words. *Thank you, Mother Earth, for healing my mate and giving Anya a second chance. Smooth out this ground so no other asks a question upon first glance.*

Warmth washed over my hands and through my body, the earth's way of repaying my thanks. With a low tremble, the ground shifted to cover the holes and erase all traces of Emerson and Anya's time there.

Standing, I turned to face the small group with some trepidation. This was new territory for me, and I felt so nervous I squeezed my hands together to keep them from trembling. But I'd made a promise to Anya, and I planned to keep it.

"Shall we?" I asked, gesturing for them to go first. I'd thought to keep my distance from Emerson, but his first step had him stumbling, and I moved instantly to his side. Wrapping one arm around his waist to support him, I felt more than heard soft laughter in my mind. *You did that on purpose, didn't you?*

He shrugged, unrepentant. *It worked, didn't it?*

Shaking my head at his antics, I continued to follow Dominic and Reese through the woods and back to town. We made our way slowly through the trees, our footsteps muffled by the soft carpet of fallen leaves and pine needles. The forest was quiet, save for the occasional chirp of a bird or rustle of a small animal in the underbrush. Despite the tranquil surroundings, I couldn't shake the feeling of unease that had settled in the pit of my stomach. I kept my senses flared, searching for any sign of our enemies, my eyes darting from shadow to shadow as we moved deeper into the woods. The air was thick with the scent of earth and green, growing things, but beneath it all, I caught the faintest whiff of something else—something dark and dangerous, like the acrid tang of smoke on the wind before a wildfire. We may not have seemed to be in any kind of rush, but I knew that time was of the essence. Every moment we spent in the open was another moment our enemies had to find us, to strike when we were at our most vulnerable. I tightened my grip on Emerson's waist, silently urging him to move faster, even as I scanned the trees for any hint of movement or sound that might betray the presence of our foes. Shadowmen, or, apparently, daemons. *Did you know of the daemon's existence?*

Dominic and Reese told me of them, he answered carefully.

You should have told me.

I didn't want you to worry more than you already were.

I don't need your protection.

He paused in his movements, cupping my cheek until I looked directly at him. His eyes were warm, sparkling like the clearest emeralds. *I will always protect you, as you will me. As mates, we can do no other. But I promise not to keep such information from you again.*

My breath hitched, and I was at a loss for words. His gaze drew me in, lighting every nerve ending with flickering flames. Blinking once, I broke the spell and sucked in a breath. He may not be as dangerous to me as shadowmen were, but the power he possessed over my will was more than terrifying.

"Let's go," I murmured aloud, shaky from the brief encounter.

Dominic and Reese were already well ahead, and I knew Emerson needed to rest. It took us the better part of an hour to hit the outskirts of town, where we paused to take in the relatively busy streets. Dominic glanced at Anya uncertainly as Emerson did his best to stand straight and appear healthy.

"Don't worry," I said. "I've got us covered."

Murmuring a quick glamour to encompass the five of us, we started off slowly through the streets, knowing anyone we came across would see two happy couples holding hands, their faces alight with love and contentment. I kept Anya completely out of the glamour for her protection and ours, ensuring that she remained invisible to prying eyes. Since I had no idea where she came from before she ended up in Maurice's clutches—and, judging by her reaction, it wasn't a happy story—I thought it best no one saw her with us. Her past was a mystery, one that I knew would unfold in time, but for now, our priority was to keep her safe and out of sight as we navigated the winding streets of the city.

It would also cause quite a commotion to see an unconscious woman being carried through town by a big and scary man.

That's a neat trick. I have much to learn from you. Emerson's praise made my chest expand with warmth. It had been a long time since I'd wanted anyone's approval. The last time would have been...my brother. *What is it? Your emotions went from glowing to incredibly sad.*

Startled by his ability to read me so easily, I answered him honestly. *I was thinking of my brother.*

His arm tightened around my shoulder, where he used me for balance. *I'm so sorry, Aurelia.*

A strange thrill shot through me whenever he used my full name. My real name. Changing the subject, I said, *Thank you for only using my nickname aloud.*

Is it all right if I use Aurelia privately? It is a beautiful name.

Thank you. And yes, that's fine. It's just...it's a part of myself I'm not ready to share with anyone else.

Through our connection, I could feel what my words meant to Emerson. He glowed now, much as I had earlier.

We arrived at the square brick building that held the hotel and used a side entrance to avoid the lobby. Reese opened one of the rooms and gestured us inside, handing off our key. "We're next door. Rest as long as you need. Let us know when you're ready—we'll make sure Anya is comfortable."

"She'll sleep through the day," I assured them. "I'll come tonight for when she wakes."

They nodded their understanding. I waited while Emerson took the key and thanked his brother before allowing me to help him into the room. Inside was a suite with one queen bed and a comfortable sitting area. The bathroom had a shower—an amenity I had missed after staying in small villages so often—and there was a good bet there was enough hot water to take a long soak.

"Would you like to lie down? Or how about a shower?" I asked, unsure of the protocol now that we were alone.

"A shower sounds perfect," Emerson said with a smile.

Helping him into the bathroom, I left him to his own devices while I checked all ingresses in the room and set my own protections. I walked the perimeter, my fingers trailing along the walls as I muttered incantations under my breath. The air shimmered faintly as the wards snapped into place, an invisible barrier against any unwanted intrusions.

There were several sets of clothes on the bed—men's clothes, which Emerson must have brought from wherever they had been staying prior to rescuing me, but also several women's items that Reese must have either purchased or loaned to me. I ran my fingers over the soft fabrics, a small smile tugging at my lips. It was a thoughtful gesture, a reminder that even in the midst of chaos, they hadn't forgotten about my needs.

It was thoughtful, and though I had a couple of outfits in my bag, all my items were, at this point, in desperate need of washing. The scent of sweat and grime clung to them, a testament to the trials we had endured. I gathered them up, making a mental note to find a laundromat or some soap to use in the bathtub as soon as possible. For now, though, the fresh clothes on the bed would more than suffice.

The bathroom door opened, and Emerson emerged with only a towel wrapped low on his hips. His appearance caught me so off-guard that I froze to the spot, unable to look away from his chiseled form. When I finally dragged my eyes to his face, he had a satisfied smirk that immediately put my teeth on edge. Grabbing the nearest pile of clothes, I threw them at his chest and glared. "Go put some clothes on."

"If that's what you really want," he replied, turning slowly to head back into the bathroom.

Crossing my arms over my stomach to contain the strange wash of emotions, I grabbed my own pile of clothes and waited for him to be done. When he opened the door again, Emerson wore a pair of drawstring pants and a t-shirt, his damp hair only adding to his appeal. Swallowing hard, I scooted past him and pointed toward the bed.

"Lay down," I ordered before shutting the door in his face.

The small semblance of privacy afforded by the closed bathroom door did nothing to calm my frayed nerves. I knew this had been a mistake from the start. I'd been surviving on my own for years, relying on no one but myself. I didn't need Emerson's smug smile or his hard, sculpted muscles distracting me from what needed to be done. I had to focus on the task at hand and not let his presence unnerve me, even though being this close to him made my heart race and my palms sweat.

If you need any help in there, I'd be happy to assist. His whispered words sent a wave of heat curling through me.

I just bet you would, I shot back, annoyed at him, at myself, and the whole situation.

Cranking the water temperature up as high as it would go, I shed the clothes that had been clinging to my body for the past three days and stepped under the scalding spray. The sensation of the steaming water cascading over my skin was nothing short of miraculous, soothing my aching muscles and washing away the grime and exhaustion. Even as I savored the blissful moment, I could still sense Emerson's presence lingering in my mind, his thoughts brushing against my consciousness like a gentle caress. Faint impressions of tantalizing images flickered through our mental connection, scenes that he seemed to be focusing on with intense concentration. I caught glimpses of his fingers trailing along my bare skin, leaving a trail of goosebumps in their wake. His mouth capturing mine in a searing kiss, our tongues tangling in a passionate dance. His lips blazing a fiery path down my neck, exploring new territories and igniting my desire. The vivid sensations sent shivers down my spine, making me ache for his touch, for the real thing rather than just a teasing mental projection.

Blinking, I snapped out of the onslaught of images with a groan. *Stop.*

His light laughter told me he had no intention of doing any such thing. *It's not too late for me to join you.*

Closing my eyes, I leaned my forehead against the cool tile, feeling overwhelmed by...everything. Emerson's obvious attraction. My own growing needs.

The fact that I could never fulfill any of it.

Tears sprang to my eyes, mixing with the shower spray as they flowed down my flushed cheeks. I'd been a naive idiot to believe I could ever have a normal life with Emerson. I wasn't normal—I wasn't an Elemental. I couldn't give Emerson my body or my blood, no matter how badly I craved to. The primal need beat at my very soul to become wholly his, to take him as my own mate for all eternity. The intoxicating scent of his blood enticed me in a way I never thought possible, awakening dark desires within. I knew how difficult it would be for Emerson to deny himself my blood in return.

It would be best for me to leave him again, to let Emerson live his life—without me as a constant temptation and danger. And yet...I couldn't bring myself to do it. I couldn't fathom leaving him, not after everything we'd been through together. That startling realization both intrigued and terrified me to my core. Was I strong enough to stay by Emerson's side without giving in to my basest Elemental urges? Or would my darkened soul ultimately tear us apart and destroy the profound love blossoming between us? I gazed unseeing at the tiled wall, my heart and mind in similar chaos as I grappled with an impossible choice.

Aurelia. The voice instantly calmed and ignited me. *Come out here. It's all right. I expect nothing of you but for you to be you.*

I sucked in a breath and then another, little hiccups shuddering through my chest in my attempt to stop the tears.

Aurelia. Huddled in the corner, I shook with the intensity of my emotions. I was a mess, too much of one to be anyone's mate. Emerson would just have to let me go.

The water shut off abruptly, leaving an eerie silence in its wake. From around the curtain, a plush robe emerged, held open invitingly for me to step into. I did so with trembling limbs, my conflicting emotions rendering me vulnerable and exposed. Emerson draped the soft, comforting cloth around my shoulders with a gentle touch, securing it snugly before carefully lifting me from the tub's embrace. Though I expected him to set me down on the cool tiles of the bathroom floor, he instead carried me through the main room with purposeful strides. He lay me tenderly on the bed, the downy comforter enveloping my shivering form. I curled into myself, body quaking from everything but the cold.

He stretched out beside me, drawing me to him with infinite tenderness. My head nestled in the niche of his neck, and I breathed in his scent. Even after three days in the earth and his recent shower, he still smelled of musk and peonies.

"Shh, it's all right, just let it out," he murmured softly, stroking my back. I realized tears were still falling, dampening his chest as they soaked through the fabric of his shirt. Though I felt ridiculous for breaking down like this, for letting my emotions overwhelm me so completely, I couldn't seem to stop the flow. The sobs kept coming, wracking my body with their intensity, and all I could do was cling to him as wave after wave of pent-up anguish poured out of me.

I'm sorry, I said into his mind instead.

No, I'm sorry. I shouldn't have teased you. I went too far.

It's not that, I tried to explain. *It's...I can't be your mate, Emerson. Not fully. Not in the way you deserve.*

He remained quiet for a time, and I let the anguish wash through me. This was it. He was going to reject me.

Silly woman, he said instead. *You are the one I want to be with. Not just because we are mates but because of who you are. Even though you refused to speak to me, we have a very strong connection. I was able to see into your mind, your strength and emotions there. You are the most incredible woman, person, I have ever met. However long you need to feel comfortable with me and our relationship, I am happy to give to you.*

Sniffing, I pulled back just enough to look into his eyes. The emerald jewels glittered down at me, filled with an emotion I was afraid to name. *Really? Even if you can't drink my blood? Even if I can't...be physical with you?*

We are being physical right now, Emerson corrected gently. *Just holding you in my arms, just like this, is all I need.*

My eyes searched his, looking for the truth in that statement. He opened himself to me, all barriers gone. I could feel what he felt— a little nervous but more excited, and something else—something that had been building since the moment our eyes had met in that tavern.

Love.

It flowed over and through him, engulfing me in its bright light. I felt breathless with the intensity of it, the utter honesty of it. Before I could stop myself, I reached up and met my lips to his, finally giving into the temptation there. He tasted the same way he smelled, and I ate like a woman starved.

Emerson let me lead, sensing my need for control. The kiss deepened as he coaxed my mouth open to his, our tongues dancing in a soft exchange. It lit that same fire in me, skittering along my skin and setting my blood pumping quickly through my veins.

Though my body craved more, my mind wasn't ready. I pulled back, gazing up at him in a daze. He watched me, just the same, as affected by the kiss as I. It felt at once like I'd been bulldozed flat and as if I flew through the clouds. Into the silence, I finally said, "I'll try. I don't know how long it will take, but I'll try."

"Thank you," Emerson replied, kissing the tip of my nose. Pressing his lips against my forehead next, he added, "For giving me your trust."

My heart settled at his words, and I allowed my eyes to slide closed. Though the future remained an unknown void, for the moment—wrapped in Emerson's arms—I felt optimistic about what was to come. For the first time in three days, I slept.

$$Chapter\ 12$$

When I woke, the sun had already dipped low in the western sky, casting a warm, golden glow across the landscape. I lay still, savoring the peaceful moment. I hadn't moved, and neither had Emerson. His strong arms were still wrapped protectively around me, holding me close to his muscular chest. My head rested against him, rising and falling with each steady breath he took. Oddly, I didn't feel constricted or trapped by his embrace—instead, I felt cozy and content, as if I was exactly where I was meant to be. A sense of belonging and rightness suffused me, and I snuggled even closer, letting out a contented sigh. For this perfect, tranquil moment, all was right in the world.

With a start, I realized my sleep had been peaceful and nightmare-free. I honestly couldn't remember the last time I'd slept without interruption. The only difference had been that I lay in Emerson's arms, protected by his innate strength.

His arms flexed, pulling me somehow tighter against him, and I knew he'd woken. My eyes fluttered open, pulling back just enough to look into his eyes. "Good morning."

"Good morning," he said, his voice deep and filled with sleep. The whispered words reminded me of our daily one-sided conversations.

"We slept the day away," I replied with a half-smile. "I hope that's not your usual habit."

"I would remain here forever as long as you were in my arms."

Rolling my eyes, I slapped playfully against his broad shoulders, though I had little wiggle room. "I'm here; you can stop sweet-talking me now."

He grinned wickedly; his thoughts were clear on his face. "Never."

Bending down to place his lips against my throat, I stiffened against the contact. Not that I wanted to move away—no, I wanted so much more—but because I feared he would get carried away and allow his incisors to lengthen.

Instead, he feathered kisses along my jaw, moving slowly and leisurely until he met my mouth. I relaxed into the kiss gladly, enjoying the awakening of cells his touch caused. "Mm, definitely not moving."

Letting out half a laugh, I struggled to sit up. "We have to. I promised I would be there when Anya woke."

Propping up against his elbows, Emerson watched me quietly for a few moments until I turned self-conscious. Tugging at my hair,

I realized I'd fallen asleep with it wet, not even brushing through it first. I must look like a wreck.

"You're beautiful," Emerson said with such intensity I completely forgot what I had been doing.

"I'm glad you think so," I replied flippantly. "No one else would take on this mess."

"If anyone tried, they would have me to answer to." Though his tone was light, I could tell he was dead serious. It should have made me rebel, to assert my independence, but it only served to make me feel cherished. Switching topics, he said, "Dominic and Reese are ready whenever we are."

"All right, but I think I need to try that shower thing again—I didn't do a very good job yesterday."

His devilish grin had me scurrying into the other room, closing and locking the door behind me with a resounding click. Not that it mattered when he could turn into mist and slip through the tiniest of cracks, but it gave me a semblance of privacy and control, a fleeting moment to gather my thoughts.

Moving quickly, I stepped into the shower, letting the warm water cascade over my skin and wash away the remnants of the previous night. After a few minutes of luxuriating under the spray, I reluctantly turned off the water and wrapped myself back in the plush robe, the soft fabric caressing my skin.

When I stepped into the main room, Emerson had already dressed in clean clothes, his emerald eyes sparkling with mischief as he watched me enter. Grabbing a pile of neatly folded garments that Reese had thoughtfully left for me, I returned to the bathroom to change, the cool tiles beneath my feet sending a shiver up my spine.

Combing through my hair with gentle strokes, I secured the long blonde tresses in a loose braid, the silky strands gliding through my fingers like golden threads. With a final glance in the mirror, I took a deep breath and returned to Emerson's side, ready to face whatever the day had in store for us.

Reese had left me a dress—it would be difficult to guess pant sizes, I supposed—and I felt insecure as I walked back into the main room. The baby blue almost perfectly matched my eyes, while delicate white roses scattered along the skirt.

When Emerson's gaze landed on me, his eyes darkened, smoldering with intensity. His lashes sank halfway down, creating a sultry, sexy expression. "You look amazing."

"Thanks," I replied uncertainly, my throat unusually dry. Lifting out the skirt and letting it drop, I felt the need to explain, "Reese left me clothes. It was thoughtful of her. Not really my style, though."

Emerson held out a hand, which I accepted after just the briefest pause. "Remind me to thank Reese, as well."

Though my initial reaction was to roll my eyes again, I got caught and held in his emerald gaze. He didn't move, didn't speak, and yet I floundered like a fish in a net, trapped and unable to breathe.

"Let's go," Emerson finally said. He didn't release my hand as he opened the door and started down the hall. I hadn't noticed much of the hotel last night, but it had a beautiful, old-world architecture that I found charming.

Has Dominic found any more traces of the shadowman you have been hunting?

Not since we left the mountains, Emerson answered. We spoke privately now that we were out of the protective shield I'd had around the room. *We thought he might be with the group led by Maurice, but he eluded us again.*

Did you have an idea of where to go next?

Not yet. We'll speak more about it with Dominic and Reese. Is there somewhere you wish to go?

Hesitating for a moment before answering, I finally said, *I was heading toward one of my larger caches on the eastern edge of Russia. I would still like to go there to collect my things. Now that Maurice is gone, I think I'm done with Europe.*

I'd be happy to accompany you, Emerson said, raising the back of my hand to his lips. *We can continue searching for our elusive shadowman on the way.*

Nodding as we stopped in front of Dominic and Reese's door, I waited while Emerson knocked politely. Dominic opened the door before the knock was complete and allowed us entry. Reese sat on the edge of Anya's bed, stroking back her hair with gentle fingers. She looked up at me and smiled. "I knew that dress would look amazing on you."

"Thanks for the clothes—and everything."

"No problem," she said, then looked back to Anya. "Do you think she'll wake on her own, or do you need to wake her?"

"I'll wake her," I said, trading places with Reese. Once I was seated, I murmured another incantation and watched as her soft eyes blinked open. "Hi, Anya."

"Arie. This wasn't all a dream?"

"I'm afraid not," I said. Helping her into a sitting position, I gestured toward Dominic and Emerson, who were standing near the window, as far away as possible in the room. "That's Emerson; he's my mate. And Dominic, his brother, is Reese's mate. They won't hurt you; I promise."

Though she watched them with obvious fear, Anya nodded at me, then asked, "What happened to me?"

"It's a long story, so before I begin, do you need anything? Are you hungry, thirsty?"

"Yes," she replied, placing a hand against her throat. "Both."

I knew she would be thirsty for blood, but we would get to that. Luckily, Reese had thought ahead and asked for vegetable soup and bottles of water to be delivered. It would help make Anya comfortable for the time being.

Placing the tray of food on Anya's lap, Reese backed away again, sitting on the bottom edge of the bed while I spoke. "The men who took you were evil," I began. "And they changed you into something more than human. They did so with me, too, but that doesn't make us evil. We are something called Elementals."

"Elementals?" Anya asked, confused.

"Yes." After encouraging her to take a bite of soup, I continued, "We are a group of people with special abilities. We are able to control the elements, have great speed and power, and we live a long time."

"This sounds like superheroes," Anya said, wanting to laugh as if it wasn't true. "Or...vampires."

I smiled gently before answering. "We're more like vampires."

"You mean..." She held her throat again, her eyes wide and glassy. "That's the thirst I feel?"

"Yes," I said, not wanting to sugarcoat. "You will need to drink blood to survive and be at full power—but we don't kill anyone."

Her gaze flicked from me to Reese, over Emerson and Dominic, and back again. I waited for her to process, knowing how shocking all of this could be. "When I was a little girl, I dreamt of a world where I could be strong. I dreamt of a prince on a white horse. He was strong and courageous and rescued me from the bad men."

She focused down at the bowl of soup, an ageless look in her eyes. I realized that though this woman was young in years, she had seen more than anyone ever should. Summoning any compassion that I possessed, I placed my palm against her arm. "It's okay. You don't have to talk about it if you don't want to."

She nodded her thanks, then ate another spoonful. My heart broke as I realized that Maurice wasn't the first monster she'd faced. My eyes met Emerson's as complete understanding passed between us. This was a young, beautiful, probably orphaned girl in Russia. Her story would not be a happy one.

Reese's cell phone buzzed, and she excused herself to answer it. Emerson took a few steps closer, speaking to Anya directly. "Anya, I'm Emerson. You are under our protection now. You can remain with us as long as you'd like. If you have somewhere else that you'd like to go, we will get you there safely."

She watched him for a few moments, judging his words. "I have nowhere to go."

"We will help you, then. We will teach you about your new powers, and if at any time you decide to leave us, we will understand. You will never be a prisoner again."

"Thank you," she said quietly. When she finished her soup, she looked back at me. "I would like to go outside. I have spent too much of my life locked up."

"Of course," I said, smiling. "Let's go discover some of your powers."

Reese came back into the room, handed Anya some clothes, and showed her to the bathroom so she could shower. Once we were alone in the room, Reese told us about her phone call.

"That was Jace; he will be arriving tomorrow. We can ask Anya if she'd like him to look at her. Emerson, how are you feeling?"

"Perfect, though we will need to feed soon," he said, including me in his statement.

Reese nodded. "So will Anya. We'll have to see if she'll be comfortable feeding from one of us."

Emerson approached me as I stood, placing his palm against my lower back. I soaked in his strength, knowing the long road we had ahead. "Have the two of you thought any about where you'd like to go from here?"

They shared a sheepish look before Reese answered. "We can't really decide. I love to travel—it's what I've done my entire adult life— but Dominic wants to settle down somewhere."

"Arie would like to stop in eastern Russia, but after that, we would both be happy to leave Europe," Emerson said.

"What about the shadowman you've been hunting for?" Reese asked. Emerson and Dominic shared a look this time.

"We have more important things to look after now," Emerson replied, slipping his arm fully around my waist and tightening his grip.

"We will continue to hunt shadowmen, but I, for one, would like to start my new life with my mate. And you two need to do the same, if not for yourselves, then for your children."

Reese reached out and clasped Dominic's hand, a silent understanding flowing between them. Before we could say anything more, Anya emerged from the bathroom, looking refreshed. She also wore a pretty sundress, though I could tell she felt as uncomfortable as I did in the outfit.

"We'll go shopping for some new clothes," I promised her. "We're in Omsk. Do you know anyone here? Do we need to hide you from view?"

"No," she said, shaking her head. "I am from Ryazan, just outside of Moscow. We shouldn't run into any of the bad men here."

"Okay. Before we go, we were wondering if you would try drinking blood from one of us. You need your strength after your conversion, and it might be easier to start with someone you know."

"I would be happy to volunteer. I am Dominic, and you are under my protection, as well."

After taking a deep breath, Anya latched onto me but nodded. "You will be near?"

"Yes. I know it sounds distasteful, but you won't be hurting Dominic. He'll let you know when you've had enough."

Dominic walked over to us, casually biting into his own wrist and offering it to Anya. She cringed away initially but then leaned forward to sniff at his offering. Letting out a little laugh of surprise, she said, "This smells…good."

"That's okay," I said. "It should. I know it's strange, but it's how we survive."

Keeping her eyes locked on mine, she maneuvered until she could grip Dominic's wrist with both of her dainty hands. After another moment of hesitation, she placed her lips over the twin dots, adjusting to the taste before taking a pull. I kept a reassuring smile on my face, nodding encouragingly when she paused. She lifted her head, confusion clouding her expression. "It tastes good."

"It's all right. Go on, keep drinking."

Nodding, she bent her head to the task once more, her cheeks flushing with color as she reached her fill. The rich, intoxicating taste of Dominic's blood filled her senses, and a pleasant warmth spread through her body. She drank deeply, savoring every drop until Dominic gently let her know when she'd had enough. Reluctantly, she pulled away, her lips stained crimson. She stepped back, a dazed look on her face as she tried to process the overwhelming sensations. "Thank you," she murmured, her voice soft and slightly breathless.

"Anytime," he answered.

"All right," I said. "Let's go find out what you can do."

Chapter 13

We walked at a human pace back into the mountains. Once we reached the outskirts of town, Reese turned to Emerson and me. "If Anya feels comfortable with us, you two can go feed and meet us after."

"That would be all right," Anya agreed. It amazed me how well she acclimated to her new life. It made me wonder just how bad her life had been before this.

"Thank you," Emerson said to Reese. "We will meet you shortly."

Reese turned to Anya with a grin. "Want to see how fast you can run?"

She nodded excitedly, and before I could blink, the three of them disappeared into the trees. We watched for a moment before Emerson offered me his arm. "Shall we?"

This time, I didn't hesitate. Looping my hand through the crook of his elbow, I allowed myself to be swept up in the moment. For the briefest of instances, I felt like what I imagined a normal woman must feel like on a date with a handsome man. Lighthearted, carefree, happy. Human. It was a fleeting sensation but one I clung to desperately, savoring the warmth of his arm beneath my fingers and the way my heart fluttered in my chest. For just a heartbeat, I let myself forget the darkness that haunted my past and the uncertainty that clouded my future and simply reveled in the present.

We walked slowly back through town, finding a group of men leaving a restaurant. Emerson called out a greeting, asking for directions before leading them around the corner of the building. I cast a spell so that no one could see what we were doing and stepped up to one of the men.

Murmuring an incantation to blur his memory, I lifted his wrist and had my incisors poised to sink into his vein when I sensed danger. Glancing up, to my surprise, the feeling came from Emerson. He glared at the man I'd been about to feed from, his hard gaze frightening me.

"Emerson? What is it?" I asked, a tremble in my voice.

"Step away from him, please," Emerson replied, his words ground out from a tight jaw.

I released the man's wrist like I'd been burned and took a few steps back, confused and a little hurt. Self-conscious, yet again. I hated feeling that way. "What did I do wrong?"

Emerson's eyes snapped to mine, the fiery gaze softening once he recognized my expression. He sighed in frustration. "I'm sorry. That was a new feeling for me."

Luckily, he'd already cast a hazy spell on the other men, so our conversation remained relatively private. "What feeling?"

"Jealousy," he said, shaking his head with a self-deprecating smile. "I've never felt jealousy before, but to watch you put your mouth on that man...."

I looked at the man leaning heavily against the wall and back to Emerson. "You were...jealous?"

"I'm so sorry," he repeated. "I know it's silly, and yet...I can't stop. Could you...would you feed from me once I feed from them?"

A short laugh burst from my throat, surprising us both. When was the last time I'd laughed? I honestly couldn't remember. Slapping a hand over my mouth, I said, "Sorry! I'm not laughing at you, exactly. Just the situation. Um, sure, I'll wait."

His mouth pressed together in a thin line, but when he spoke into my mind, I could hear the humor there. *I can't believe you're laughing at me, woman.*

Hurry up, caveman, I replied. *I want to get back to Anya.*

Emerson shook his head but bent to the task, taking his fill from the three men before releasing them. He left money in their pockets, knowing it was something I liked to do. *I never told you that.*

It was in your memories.

You'll have to teach me that trick.

It should have felt like an invasion of privacy. But somehow, I felt okay with Emerson running around in my thoughts. In response, he wrapped his arms around my waist and placed his lips against the base of my throat. It sent tingles down my spine, and I felt like liquid against his hard frame.

Before I realized what he planned to do, Emerson lifted us into the air, floating above the town and back toward the mountains. *Feed, Aurelia. Take what you need.*

The world around us blurred into an indistinct haze until only Emerson remained. His scent wafted over me, an intoxicating aroma so enticing that my mouth practically watered in anticipation of the exquisite taste of him on my lips. Leaning in, I nuzzled against the warm skin of his neck, feeling the vibration of his low groan. A thrill ran through me, enjoying the heady knowledge that I alone had the capability of riling him up, of stoking the flames of his desire.

Woman, you'll be the death of me.

I smirked, then sank my teeth deep, letting the first taste of Emerson roll across my tongue and savoring his essence before taking another pull. His blood tasted sweet, with that same underlying flowery aroma as his scent. It hit my veins and began to buzz, an odd sort of daze descending over my brain. Though I'd never been drunk, I imagined this is how it would have felt.

Emerson pulled me tighter against him as he let out a soft moan, and I knew he felt the same sensations as I did. I hadn't known it could be like this. Taking blood had always been a distasteful task, one that I abhorred and put off as long as possible. With Emerson, it would never be enough. His taste was now my addiction.

Taking one last pull as our feet touched the ground, I swept my tongue across the pinpricks to close the wound and took another moment just to breathe. When my eyes finally opened, my dazed look mirrored in his. "Wow. I had no idea."

"Neither did I," he said shakily, his arms still securely around my waist.

Pressed so tightly against him as I was, I could feel how I affected him. Though I thought I should be embarrassed, it was impossible at that moment. His lids lowered, and he bent to capture my mouth with his, the kiss somehow gentle and passionate at the same time. In my blissful haze, I didn't resist but rode the wave with him, reveling in the moment.

He pulled away and brushed his thumb gently under one eye, then pressed his lips to my forehead. The action alone made me feel important, cherished. I held onto him even tighter, not wanting the moment to end. Through our connection, I could feel his heart slowing, strumming out a steady beat that perfectly matched the rhythm of mine.

If this was how I felt just taking his blood, what would happen if we were to be truly together? The idea both excited and terrified me. Tipping my head back to look into those gorgeous eyes of his, I said, "We should go find the others."

"All right," he agreed. "How would you like to travel?"

"Let's run. Probably be best to keep our clothes on."

With a wink, I stepped away and headed in the direction I knew Dominic, Reese, and Anya to be. *Saucy woman. You're playing with fire.*

Grinning, I reached out and clasped his hand, running through the forest at preternatural speed. The earth sent me messages, leading me directly to our group. I knew Emerson received the same signals, which would be a new sensation for him.

Perhaps Dominic had been right about my connection being more than just an Elemental perk. *It's amazing. She's telling me everything. Has it always been like this for you?*

Ever since I escaped Maurice. She led me to the cave, where I spent a lot of time healing and learning. The place I'll take you to in a few days.

It's truly something special. A blessing.

Slowing as we reached the group, I glanced at Emerson to make sure he appeared respectable after our explosive moment in the air. His appearance was immaculate, and the grin he directed my way made my pulse flutter. *Stop that.*

Stop what?

Looking at me like I'm the most important thing in the world.

You're the most important thing in my world, he answered without hesitation.

Though it warmed me all over, I rolled my eyes at him for good measure. *Sweet talker.*

He bent down to brush his lips over the spot just below my ear. "And sweet kisser," he whispered, his breath at my ear sending chills down my spine.

"Hey guys, you made it!" Reese called out, saving Emerson from retribution.

We joined the others in the middle of a small clearing, where Reese and Dominic were showing Anya some basic exercises to hone her new abilities. She looked up as we stepped closer, her face lit in a smile. "This is amazing. I have always felt weak, like a prisoner with no control. Now I feel strong. Like I could take on the world."

"You'll have to take on that pile of dirt first," Reese said with a grin, pointing at the small mound at their feet. "We're working on manipulation."

"Come here," I said to Anya, kneeling beside it and digging my hands into the earth. "Mother Earth accepted you as her child after your conversion, as she accepted Emerson. You will have a stronger connection to her than the other elements. If you listen, you can hear her heartbeat. She will tell you all kinds of secrets if you pay attention."

Anya immediately knelt beside me and copied my movements, digging her own hands under the soil. "It helps me feel grounded. What do I do now?"

"Close your eyes and concentrate. Talk to her."

"What do I say?"

"Thank her for accepting you."

Anya closed her eyes and focused. "Thank you, Mother Earth. I promise not to squander this second chance you've given me." Silence settled over our group while we waited for Anya to speak again. Her eyes popped open as she looked at me in surprise. "I can hear it! The heartbeat."

"That's great! What else?"

Her eyebrows drew together as she continued to listen. "There are deer to the east. I know how far away each tree is, where to find the best healing herbs. I'm even connected to each of you." She looked at Reese. "You're pregnant with twin girls. They are extremely powerful." We all stared at her in shock, and as Anya registered our expressions, she began to look sheepish. "Should I not know that?"

"No, it's fine," Reese said. "It's just a surprise. I mean, I knew I was pregnant, but that the earth told you that...that's crazy awesome."

Anya frowned, her eyes going slightly hazy. Her hands were still deep in the earth, and I watched her curiously. "There is a man. He needs help."

"Where?" I asked, on instant alert.

"Not here," she said, shaking her head, her eyes clearing. She looked at me in question. "I could feel his pain. It was calling to me, but it's gone now."

"I'm sorry, that's new to me," I said, looking between the others. They seemed baffled as well. "Were you able to find out anything more? Who he is, or where he is?"

"No," she said, standing. "But I sent him good thoughts."

Sensing she didn't want to discuss it further, I said, "All right. What else would you like to learn?"

∞ ∞ ∞

THE HEALER ARRIVED THE NEXT evening, and I still debated whether or not I even wanted to meet him. Reese seemed to trust that he could help her, and I knew that Anya was curious about him as well. Since she had been recently converted, I wondered if she had a better chance of eradicating Maurice from her soul.

If such a thing were even possible.

Dominic had gotten Anya her own room, as she had to stay out of the sun like I did. Once the sun had dipped below the horizon, I knocked on her door. Emerson waited for me in our room until I made my decision.

"Hello, Anya," I greeted the young woman when she opened the door. "How are you feeling?"

She stepped back to allow me entry before answering. "I'm in pain, but it's manageable. How are you?"

"Same," I said with a smile. "But I've been living with it for years, so I hardly think about it anymore. I wanted to talk to you about the healer."

"Yes." She nodded, perching on the edge of the bed. "I decided I would like to meet him."

Trying to withhold my trepidation, I asked, "Are you sure?"

"If he can help, yes."

"I'm hoping since you didn't receive Maurice's blood directly, that it doesn't have as much a hold on you as it does me. Reese seems to believe highly in this man—so if that's your decision, I support it."

She let out a little breath. Before we'd rested for the day, we'd had a long talk about Maurice and what had actually happened to her. Why she felt a gnawing pain at all times. She took it much better than I had expected and even thanked me for saving her. I didn't deserve her gratitude, but I also knew that I couldn't prevent her from trying to get healed.

She still seemed nervous, though, so I steeled myself for making the right decision. "Why don't you let me meet him first, just to make sure he's trustworthy?"

Her eyes shot up to mine, wide and hopeful. "Really? You would do that?"

"Yes. Emerson and I will go now, and then I'll come right back." On impulse, Anya wrapped her arms around me in a hug, taking me by surprise. I wasn't much for physical contact—except now with Emerson—but I pat her back lightly in return. "I'll be right back."

Emerson kept in contact with his brother through their own telepathic link, so we knew Jace had arrived and had already examined Reese and her babies.

I'd like to meet the healer, I sent to Emerson. Within seconds, he arrived at my side.

Holding out his hand, he gave me a reassuring smile. "Let's go."

Clasping his hand, I took a deep breath and followed him back up to the third floor. Though I felt nervous, I took comfort in the fact that Dominic—one of the most overprotective people on earth—had trusted Jace enough to examine Reese. When we reached the door, Emerson knocked while I shifted my weight from foot to foot and placed my hands in position to quickly grab weapons.

Emerson didn't comment, but he did move his hand to my lower back. It was his way of showing solidarity without getting in my way. It should have frightened me, how in tune we seemed to be, yet it only served to reassure me.

Dominic answered within seconds, greeting us both with a nod. Emerson entered the room first, partially shielding me from view. Reese sat in a chair, her hands over her stomach, while the stranger stood a few feet away.

"Emerson, nice to meet you," the man said, perfectly politely. He had close-cropped black hair and when his gaze landed on me, I found myself rooted to the spot. His eyes were shock blue, a color I'd only seen once before.

On Maurice.

"You must be Arie," he said. His tone remained gentle, and he kept his distance. I stiffened anyway.

Aurelia? What is it?

The eyes...his eyes....

Emerson's narrowed at the stranger, trying to see what I saw. In an instant, he shielded me completely from view. "I apologize; it seems we will not be able to stay. Dominic?"

Dominic nodded stiffly. This told me Emerson explained to him privately what had happened. I didn't care as long as I didn't have to spend another second in this room. We backed out, and I caught a reassuring smile from Dominic before the door closed. Without a word, Emerson led me away and back to our room.

Once inside the relative safety of the room, I sank to the floor with my head in my hands. My heart beat double its normal pace, and I felt disgusted with myself. Once the terror of the moment ceased, I knew I would be angry, too. But only with myself.

Always myself.

Emerson crouched before me.

"I'm sorry," I murmured. "I'm so sorry."

"Aurelia." Emerson said my name sternly, waiting for me to make eye contact before speaking again. "You have nothing to apologize for. I told you that you would have my support no matter what you decided, and you do. All right?"

Studying his features as he spoke, I nodded and allowed him to help me to my feet. "I just hate feeling weak. Fear makes me weak."

"Silly woman," Emerson said with a gentle smile. "You are the strongest person I know. Being afraid doesn't change that."

My heart settled at his words, finding and matching the rhythm of his. Laying my head against his shoulder, I took deep breaths until Emerson's calm washed over me. "I promised Anya I would go right back to her. I'm not sure if she'll have the same reaction to Jace as I did."

"I'll ask Dominic to have Reese go talk to her. She can explain what happened and leave it up to Anya to decide." I nodded, still shaky from the unexpected encounter. Emerson studied me carefully while he communicated with his brother. "I know what we should do," he said suddenly. Taking my hand, he walked over to the window overlooking the city and lifted it a few inches. "Follow my lead."

With his eyes on mine, Emerson slowly dissolved into the air itself, slipping through the crack and re-forming into the shape of a hawk. Before joining him, I murmured a spell to protect our room and belongings, then gave myself over to nothingness.

Once out in the cool air, I formed into a slightly smaller version of Emerson's bird, spreading my wings out into the night. We flew toward the mountains, moving at a leisurely pace, allowing the air currents to catch and carry us across the sky.

I'd always found more freedom in flying than anything else I'd ever done, the sensation of the wind rushing past my feathers and the world sprawling out beneath me filling me with a sense of limitless possibility. I understood that Emerson gave me a precious gift by encouraging our little jaunt, a chance to escape the worries and cares that weighed us down. Spiraling under and around Emerson playfully, I let out a joyful cry, knowing he needed this carefree moment as much as I did. There hadn't been a lot of fun or lightness in his life, not since the innocence of childhood had been stripped away. But here, soaring through the star-flecked night sky together, we could begin to re-learn how to embrace happiness, to find hope and healing in the simple joy of each other's company.

Thank you, I sent to him.

For what?

For allowing me to be me. For understanding. And for giving me this.

Anytime.

We flew far from civilization, deep into the wilds of Russia. When we decided the time had come to head back, I reversed direction and aimed for the ground, transforming at the last moment into the shape of a wolf. From Emerson's stories, I knew that the wolf was his preferred animal. After everything he'd done for me, I could give him this.

Emerson's massive wolf materialized before my eyes, his russet coat gleaming in the dappled sunlight that filtered through the forest canopy. His powerful form moved with a grace that belied his size, his speed leaving me in awe. My own wolf, though more compact and lithe, with a pelt of burnished tawny hues, rose to the challenge, determined to match him stride for stride.

We surged forward as one, our paws pounding against the earth in a rhythmic cadence as we wove through the labyrinth of trees. Fallen logs and moss-covered boulders posed no obstacle, our agile bodies sailing over them with effortless ease. The occasional stream intersected our path, and we plunged through the cool, crystal waters, sending glittering droplets cascading in our wake.

Whenever Emerson drew too near, I'd wheel around, my jaws snapping playfully at his haunches, a teasing reminder that I wouldn't be so easily caught. Laughter bubbled up within me, a pure, unadulterated joy at the freedom to simply exist in this moment, my heart full to bursting with the love and companionship of my mate running steadfastly at my side.

It had become so automatic for me to allow my senses to flare out, always on alert, that I didn't even realize I was doing it. Every touch of padded paw to earth sent me signals—where other wildlife grazed or played, the lack of people. The wind against my fur told me what weather would come next and whispered secrets into my ears.

This had become so second nature that when a resounding beat echoed against my skull, I stumbled, rolling along the ground until I came to rest against my side. My huge head shook in disbelief, distrust.

What I had heard could not be real.

Aurelia! Emerson's concerned cry shouted into my mind. *What is it?*

Forcing myself up off the ground, I focused everything I had on that discordant beat. It couldn't be true. And yet, when I put out all my feelers, what I found was unmistakable. Without answering Emerson, I took off like a shot and found an unerring path to my target. Part of me wanted to shout with overwhelming joy, while the rest of me expected a trap.

Getting closer to the target, I finally spoke to Emerson, knowing he felt confused and concerned. *Stay back for now.*

I can't do that, he replied immediately. *If there is danger, I will be by your side.*

I'd slowed my pace, each step deliberate and wary as I crept forward. The terrain grew rockier, and I spotted a small natural overhang jutting out from the hillside ahead. It offered scant protection to the person dwelling beneath its stony lip. My heart raced with anticipation and trepidation as I drew closer, knowing what I would find but having difficulty believing. The air seemed to hum with tension, and every sense strained to detect any hint of danger lurking in the shadows. Only when I determined the coast was clear did I respond. *Please. You will frighten her.*

Emerson stilled, and I felt him hovering in my mind, trying to ascertain my thoughts. Thankfully, he understood the urgency in my voice and respected my abilities enough to listen to my plea. The small, frail woman who looked younger than me lay on her side, curled into a ball. Her long, jet-black hair had become a tangled mess, spread across the ground. Though her eyes were closed, I knew the deep umber color better than my own.

Pulling myself into my natural form, I asked the earth to cloak my nakedness. A gentle breeze caressed my skin where the soft shirt and pants didn't cover. I approached the huddled figure with cautious steps, bare feet treading lightly on the damp soil. In a voice barely above a whisper, I called out to her, my tone soothing and full of concern. "Edith?"

Chapter 14

The huddled form remained motionless, giving no indication that it had heard my approach or my words. Undeterred, I crept closer, my footsteps soft against the earth. Kneeling beside the still figure, I tried again, my voice gentle but insistent. "Edith, it's me, Arie. I can help you."

She lifted her head, though I could see what a struggle it was. I sighed with relief as her lashes fluttered open. Her voice cracked, but she spoke. "Arie?"

"Yes, it's me. I didn't know you'd survived, but I'm here now. I can help you."

Her eyes squeezed shut, moisture leaking from the corners and trailing down her dirt-smudged cheeks. A soft whimper escaped her lips as she struggled to sit up, her movements slow and painful. I reached out to steady her, my hands gentle on her shoulders as I helped her into a sitting position. She leaned heavily against me, her breathing ragged and shallow. "Please...I want to die."

My heart broke at her utter helplessness, knowing how she had come to be in this position. For a moment, I found myself back in that darkened prison, rotting away until Maurice decided to torture me. Rape me. My only hope in that time had been this woman, who whispered to me through the bars of our shared prison. We'd kept each other alive, only to lose each other when we'd tried to escape.

I'm with you. Emerson's voice rushed through me like a breath of fresh air, pushing out the darkness and replacing it with his goodness, his love. Using his strength, I knelt beside the woman I considered my sister and placed my palm against her cheek. "Maurice is gone from this world. We are finally free. I can help you. Please, let me help you."

I could sense the war going on inside of her, her complete hopelessness battling with a sharp survival instinct we all possessed. After several long moments, she nodded her head and slipped back into unconsciousness. My gaze shot to Emerson, seeking out his light and strength in the darkness. He had shifted into his natural form, those emerald eyes reassuring and understanding.

I'll carry her back to the hotel. Will you keep us from view?

Of course, he answered instantly. *She is under my protection now, too.*

With a grateful nod, I scooped the slight woman into my arms and began to run, trusting Emerson to cover us. Edith remained passed out for the entire journey, which was probably for the best. She had come to the end of her considerable strength.

We reached the hotel in record time, and I didn't slow my frantic pace as I raced up the stairs, taking them two at a time in my desperation to reach our room. Emerson, sensing my urgency, beat me to the door, swiftly unlocking it and holding it open for me to rush inside. With quick, efficient movements, he pulled back the blankets on the bed, and I laid Edith down gently, taking care not to jostle her injured body. I covered her with the blankets, tucking them snugly around her, and then hurried to the closet to grab more, piling them on top of her shivering form. I knew she would need to feed soon to replenish her strength and accelerate her healing, but for now, the warmth of the blankets would help to begin the process.

Pulling a chair close to her bedside, I sat down and gripped one of her cold hands in both of mine, rubbing it gently to try to bring some heat back into her skin. With my other hand, I reached out and soothed across her forehead, brushing back the sweat-dampened strands of her hair in tender caresses. I couldn't take my eyes off her pale, still face, my heart clenching with worry and fear. Looking over to Emerson, who hovered anxiously nearby, I bit my lip as I considered his presence in the room, wondering if I should ask him to give us some privacy.

I will keep my distance, but I am staying, he said before I could form my thoughts into words.

Though my initial reaction was to argue, I nodded instead and focused back on Edith's pale face. *I know the best thing would be to ask the healer to examine her, but I just can't. I know she would feel the same as I do.*

Before Emerson could reply, Edith's eyelashes lifted, and for a moment, panic set in. Then she latched onto me, and confusion clouded her face. "Arie? What happened? Where am I?"

"I found you. You're at a hotel, safe now."

She pulled in a breath before nodding again, her eyes flicking over to where Emerson stood. Through my grip on her hand, I could feel her pulse begin to race.

"Shh, it's all right," I assured her. "This is Emerson, and he is not a shadowman. He is an Elemental, a race of extraordinary people. You have contact with me, see that what I say is the truth. I trust him with my life."

That admission alone would put Edith at ease, but she could also see it with her unique gift. Though her fear still showed on her face, her pulse began to slow.

"Hello, Edith," he said softly, remaining well away. "I would never harm you or allow harm to come to you. You need to feed, and I offer freely."

Edith switched her gaze back to me, weighing her decision heavily. I knew if she allowed herself to 'read' him that she would see the truth in what he said—but trusting a male to be so close would be a huge step.

It seemed we all held our breath as Edith made her decision.

You will stay right there? Edith asked, her physical touch giving her the ability to speak into my mind.

As long as you need.

She looked at Emerson head-on. "You will allow me to read you?"

"Yes," he replied without hesitation. "Whatever will make you feel more comfortable."

When Edith nodded, Emerson moved in slow, meticulous steps toward the bed. Edith's grip tightened slightly on my hand, but otherwise, she remained still. Emerson thought I was brave, but I had nothing on this woman.

Emerson reached my side and offered his hand, still keeping a healthy distance between them. Edith released her grip on me and hesitated only briefly before clasping his. Her eyes went wide, then closed, the air thickening in the room as her power hummed. As connected to Emerson as I'd become, I could hear the echo of her words when she spoke into his mind.

You are a good man. Arie deserves to be happy. Unshed tears lined the edges of Emerson's eyes as he nodded his thanks. I wondered if, with his unusually strong psychic gifts, the reading had been two-way. Lifting his wrist to his mouth, he bit into it and offered it again to Edith.

"I offer freely," he repeated, then added, "sister."

My heart swelled as I watched Edith accept his offering. She gripped his wrist between her hands and drank deeply, politely sealing the wound when she was done. Her eyes heavy with sleep, she murmured, "Thank you. I think I need to rest now."

"I'll be here when you wake," I promised. "No harm will come to you here."

She nodded, then allowed her lids to slide closed.

"I've let Dominic know what's happened," Emerson said quietly. "Reese and Anya are on their way."

I looked up from watching Edith's face, dipping my head in thanks. "If you would like to catch up with your brother and the healer, that would be all right."

"That is what I'll do."

"Tell him—tell him I'm sorry, and it's nothing personal."

"You have nothing to be sorry for, but I will relay the message just the same," Emerson said as a sharp rap echoed from the entrance, reverberating through the quiet room. With a swift motion, he pulled the heavy wooden door open, revealing Reese and Anya on the other side. The two women stepped inside with unhurried, graceful movements, their footsteps soft against the polished floor. As they entered, each offered me a subtle smile, their lips curving upwards in a gentle, reassuring gesture. The air seemed to still as they moved further into the room, their presence bringing a sense of calm and purpose to the tense atmosphere.

I will be back shortly, Emerson said. *Call if you need anything.*

Thank you.

"I will see you ladies later," he said aloud for the benefit of Reese and Anya.

They both approached the bed with cautious steps, the gravity of the situation weighing heavily upon them. Reese gently lowered herself onto the bottom edge of the mattress, the springs creaking slightly beneath her weight. Anya, her movements graceful and fluid, climbed up beside Edith's still form, settling in close to the unconscious woman.

With a tender touch, Anya reached out and stroked light fingers over Edith's pale forehead, brushing aside a few stray strands of long black hair. Her soft blue eyes shimmered with recognition and a hint of sadness as she spoke, her voice barely above a whisper. "I know her. She was with me when I was first captured, but she was kept from speaking, her voice silenced by our captors."

"I don't know what happened," I said thickly. Then, realizing Reese and Anya knew nothing of my past, I let out a sigh and explained. "We were held together when I was first captured. Edith had been held for nearly a century before me. Maurice took her and converted her when she was only fifteen years old. That's why she looks so young. I think something in his blood stunted her from reaching full maturity."

"How terrible for you both," Reese said, laying a hand on my arm.

"Edith has a unique ability. She can read others through touch, and it gives her a connection to speak telepathically. That's how we were able to communicate while we were held without the shadowmen knowing. We planned an escape. She—she sacrificed herself so that I might live. I thought I lost her." My voice cracked on the last sentence, and I felt tears brimming.

"You did not lose me," Edith murmured, her eyes still closed but struggling to open.

"I'm so sorry," I blubbered, squeezing her hand tight. "If I had known you were still alive...."

Her lashes slowly lifted so she could look at me as she replied, "You would have been captured again, too."

"I still would have tried."

"I know. That is why it was better you did not know." She gently squeezed my hand, her eyes traveling over Reese and up to Anya, her lips twitching into a smile. "You are all right."

"Yes, thanks to Arie. I'm Anya; it's nice to finally be able to speak to you."

"You, too. And you are?"

"Reese. My mate is Dominic, Emerson's brother. They will both watch over you, over all of us."

Edith's eyes flicked to me. "I told you there was goodness in the world."

"Yes, and now that I've found you, we'll all have it."

"You know, I always wanted sisters," Reese said. "Now I have three."

We all smiled at her, a bright and happy future nearly tangible in our thoughts. The air hummed with the promise of new beginnings and the strength of our bond as sisters. Edith's eyes sparkled with warmth as she held her hand out to Reese, palm up in a gentle invitation. "May I?"

Reese shrugged. "Of course."

She placed her hand in Edith's, and we all watched as her eyes went wide and then closed, her eyebrows furrowing as she concentrated. Reese looked concerned for a moment, but then Edith's eyes popped open, and she smiled. "You worry for nothing. Your children will be fine."

Reese's eyes went wide. "Really? How do you know?"

We all looked at their joined hands, and a light chuckle spread through the room. Laughter had been such a rarity for Edith, Anya, and me that it took us all by surprise.

"Not all babies could have survived the conversion," Edith explained. "Yours did. They would have already been half Elemental, with your mate's genes, but the fact that they converted makes them even more powerful. Right now, they are sharing their power with you. I, for one, cannot wait to meet your daughters."

Tears glittered against Reese's cheeks. "Thank you so much. You have no idea how much I've been worrying." Looking down at her hands, she laughed again and added, "Okay, maybe you do. But, oh man, I'm so relieved. So is Dominic. He can't wait to meet you."

"Perhaps after I have rested," Edith said with a soft smile.

"Yes, of course, we'll leave you in peace," Reese said.

Anya looked at me. "I let Jace examine me."

"Jace?" Edith said, a note of curiosity in her tone.

"A healer," I explained before looking at Anya. "How did it go?"

"He was able to lessen the pain but not eradicate it fully. He said he could heal my blood, but there is a shadow of Maurice in my mind and soul. All of ours."

Reese's head snapped up, and I recognized the look in her eyes. At first, when she spoke, it sounded as if she forgot we were in the room. "Body, mind, and soul. Arie, I think I know a way to help you! All of you." Our confused looks were enough to spur Reese into motion. She stood enthusiastically, using her hands to gesture as she spoke. "I was going to tell you earlier; Jade called yesterday, and she invited us all to her wedding. She's asking all Elementals to join them in October. Don't you see?"

Edith, Anya, and I exchanged baffled glances. "Not really."

"Reya will be there; she's a healer—a female one. Jade and Kate will be there, too."

"They're the ones that helped shadowmen?" I clarified.

"Yes!" exclaimed Reese. "Maybe between the three of them?"

I knew Edith and Anya were confused, but I didn't want to get into the deamon discussion right then. And though it made me nervous to let more strangers into our lives…. Looking at Edith's pale face and Anya's hopeful one, I found myself nodding my head. "All right. I'll agree to meet with them."

"And we get to go back to Wisconsin!" Reese said happily. "You wanted to get out of Europe anyway, right?"

"Is that okay with both of you?" I asked Edith and Anya.

"As far away from the darkness of our past would be perfectly fine with me," Edith answered first.

"I'm willing," Anya added.

"It's settled, then. We'll let Edith rest as long as she needs, then we'll head to eastern Russia before going to the States. Reese, I'm guessing one of you has a connection to get us all new identities?"

"Dominic and I will take care of it," she said with a confident smile.

"Okay, perfect. No matter what, we'll all be together from now on," I said, clasping both of the other women's hands, sharing a smile filled with something I dared not name.

Hope.

Chapter 15

For the next several days, Anya, Reese, and I rotated shifts watching over Edith, ensuring she was never alone. We kept a vigilant eye on her recovery, tending to her every need. Emerson took charge of making certain Edith fed each day, providing her with the sustenance required for her Elemental body to heal and regain its strength. Meanwhile, Dominic focused his efforts on procuring our travel documents, determined to secure our safe passage. As the days passed, Edith's condition improved steadily, her vitality returning with each passing hour. Anya, too, blossomed during this time, coming into her own and discovering the depths of her own resilience. Witnessing their transformations filled my heart with an overwhelming joy, the happiness so intense I feared it might burst from my chest.

My feelings for Emerson also intensified during this period, our bond deepening with every shared moment. The demanding nature of caring for Edith left us with precious little time alone together, our responsibilities taking precedence over our own desires. While I was eternally grateful for Emerson's unwavering support and endless understanding, I could feel my inner animal growing restless, yearning for the touch of her mate. The primal need simmered beneath my skin, a constant presence that threatened to boil over at any moment.

I wasn't sure if I was ready or not, but something deep down—some elemental part of myself—definitely was. So, when Edith gave us the all-clear to move on, I practically trembled with nerves.

The secluded lake I had sought refuge near in the aftermath of my escape from Maurice's clutches was tucked away in the heart of the mountains, far removed from the bustle of civilization. Its serene waters and surrounding wilderness had provided a sanctuary during those early days of freedom.

While Emerson and I prepared for our journey to my special place, Dominic secured accommodations at a hotel with a breathtaking view of the vast Sea of Okhotsk. Once I was satisfied that Anya and Edith were comfortably settled into their room, I gathered a small bag of essentials. With Emerson by my side, we set off to the northeast, our destination the tranquil shores of Jack London Lake.

When we got to the outskirts of the small town our family would stay in, we transformed into two hawks, winging our way across the night. The bag I'd brought was small enough that I grasped it with a talon while Emerson carried his in a similar fashion.

As we neared the lake, the high Bolshoy Annchag Ridge came into view, reminding me of the Alps. Even in the dark, we were able to see the stunning beauty of the snow-capped peaks.

There are still ice chunks floating in the lake, Emerson said, amused.

There will be ice until August most years, along with the snow on top of the mountains that never really melts.

It's a beautiful place.

His words were met with a strange mixture of melancholy and anguish. Though it had been a horrible time in my life, this was the place Mother Earth had shown me. A place to heal and become strong.

As we neared the lake, the majestic Bolshoy Annchag Ridge came into view, its snow-capped peaks reminiscent of the awe-inspiring Alps. The jagged silhouettes of the mountains stood out starkly against the inky night sky, their icy crowns glinting in the moonlight. Even in the encompassing darkness, the stunning beauty of the landscape was undeniable, taking our breath away. The pristine wilderness stretched out before us, untouched and untamed, beckoning us to explore its hidden wonders. We circled closer, the crisp mountain air filling our lungs, invigorating our senses, and filling us with a sense of exhilaration.

Emerson and I settled to the ground in our natural forms, the earth providing garments to cover. I put my hands out against a seemingly thick stone wall and felt my magic still holding strong. Emerson remained silent at my side, watching as I undid the spell keeping the cave as perfectly preserved as I'd left it and hidden from view.

The wall before me shimmered, then vanished, revealing a small opening to step through. I did so without hesitation, Emerson at my heels.

The small walkway widened into a vast cavern with a smooth stone floor and walls that seemed to stretch endlessly. Glittering stalactites hung from the ceiling above, their crystalline surfaces catching the faint light and casting eerie shadows across the chamber. Murmuring an incantation into my cupped hand, I conjured a ball of flickering flame. Its warm glow illuminated the strategically placed candles scattered about the room, their wicks springing to life as the fire danced from one to the next. The cavern came alive with the soft, golden radiance, revealing the intricate details carved into the ancient stone.

With the cave now in full view, I sucked in a deep breath and turned to Emerson, prepared for whatever reaction he would have. This cave had been my sanctuary for a long time while I healed from what Maurice had put me through. I had honed my skills, experimented with poisons, and created weapons here.

It was home, a place of refuge and solace during my darkest days. But the memories were bittersweet, a poignant mix of pain and healing, and I finally felt ready to say goodbye. After collecting all the things I'd stored here, I wouldn't be sad if I never saw it again. This cave had served its purpose, offering me sanctuary when I needed it most, but it was time to move on, to embrace the future that awaited me beyond these stone walls.

However, it still meant a lot to me to have Emerson in my space, and I stood nervously as he walked the perimeter slowly, touching a finger to a candle, inspecting the mattress made of soft feathers, examining the few books I'd been able to pilfer. I felt more exposed than when he'd first spoken into my mind.

"How long did you spend here?" Emerson asked, lifting a single frame to examine the photo. It contained the only picture I had of my brother—taken just before our parents had died. I would have been five in the picture, while Aden had just turned thirteen.

Maurice had kept it to taunt me with. When I escaped, it was the only thing that made it out with me.

"A little over a year," I said, looking around with new eyes to try to see what Emerson saw. His gaze never left my face, and I could feel the emotions beating at him. Sadness, for what I had been through. Anger, that he hadn't been here to help me. Pride, at what I had survived, and accomplished, on my own.

"If we have a thousand years together, I will never stop being amazed by you." Setting the frame down with utter care, he approached me slowly, reaching out to unclench my hands from the fists they'd tightened into. Lifting each hand, he placed a kiss in the exact center of each palm before holding them at our sides. "You are the most incredible person I've ever met. You are so strong it terrifies me, so intelligent it humbles me, and so loyal I wonder how I got so lucky to have you as my mate."

His words were my undoing, shattering the last of my defenses and leaving me raw and exposed. I stood rooted to the spot, my body trembling with the sheer intensity of the love I felt for him at that moment. It consumed me, filling every corner of my being until I thought I might burst from the overwhelming emotion.

He waited there patiently, his eyes soft and understanding, not asking or demanding anything of me but to simply be myself. He wished to protect me, to shield me from the harshness of the world, but he also knew that I would protect him, too. We were equals, partners in all things, ready to face whatever challenges life threw our way.

Knowing this bolstered me, allowed me to take that final step to close the gap between us. My hands lifted from his to brace against his chest, and he wrapped his around my waist. I leaned into him, rising up to meet his lips. But this time, I allowed him to lead.

His mouth consumed mine, the world around us going hazy and spinning out of control. Even the solid, unyielding earth, so strong and sure, seemed to tremble beneath my feet, mirroring the tremors that raced through my body. Emerson became my anchor, my safe harbor in the storm. His strong arms encircled me, holding me steady as the world tilted and swayed. In his embrace, I found solace and security, a refuge from the chaos that threatened to overwhelm me. I released my worries and gave him my trust, surrendering myself completely to the moment and to him. I gave him everything, holding nothing back as I lost myself in the depths of his kiss and the warmth of his touch.

Pulling my shirt over my head, Emerson took a swift intake of breath as his eyes swept down my form. I returned the favor, impatient now to feel him against me. As our clothes dropped to the floor, he lifted us from the ground and floated us to the thin mattress, landing on his back, so I sprawled against his chest. His hands began blazing a path along my bare skin, and I arched against him, needing everything he had to offer.

His mouth moved from mine, feathering kisses along my jaw and down my neck, across my shoulder and lower still. Rolling me gently to my back, he continued his ministrations as I gasped for air.

His scorching breath danced across my abdomen as I tangled my fingers in his silky hair, clinging to him desperately. His deft hands explored my body with deliberate slowness and gentleness, igniting a raging inferno of desire within me. I'd never experienced intimacy so profound, so all-consuming. My muscles coiled with tension, reaching for a pinnacle that hovered just beyond my grasp. Every nerve ending felt electrified, overwhelmed by the intensity of his touch, until I teetered on the knife's edge of pleasure and torment, unsure how much longer I could endure this exquisite torture.

Emerson...please.... I whispered into his mind, unable to speak aloud, not fully knowing what I asked for but needing it *now*.

Soon, he promised, his attention diverted.

Panting, grasping his hair, the mattress, scraping my nails along his back, doing anything I could to hold on while Emerson pushed me higher and higher, something inside me suddenly let loose, like a tidal wave crashing through every barrier in my body. Emerson gripped my hips and rode it out with me, satisfaction rolling from him.

But he wasn't done. He moved back until his mouth was on mine, and I felt him at my entrance. He moved unfailingly slow and gentle, allowing me to adjust and ensuring my comfort.

Fire consumed me, licked along my skin and flowed through my veins. The first explosion hadn't been enough. I needed more; I needed what only Emerson could give me. He had unleashed my inner animal, and she wouldn't be sated so easily.

He began to move, his body above mine. It felt amazing, wonderful, incredible. It felt...like I couldn't breathe. Like being choked. Trapped. Being forced against my will. I didn't want this, but I couldn't stop it. Maurice was an evil, horrible creature. His rancid taste filled my mouth, his wicked, taunting laugh ringing in my ears.

My fingers turned to claws as I thrashed and fought against the monster holding me down, tears streaming down my cheeks as I screamed helplessly.

"Aurelia!" came a husky voice, tearing through the darkness. Still, I struggled violently, lost in the dark depths of my own mind—my own memories. I felt air against my back instead of the ground—a freedom in the realization alone—as Emerson's frantic pleas finally broke through. "Aurelia, please, baby, come back to me. It's all right, you're safe. You're safe, you're safe."

Emerson's strong arms encircled me, holding me close as I shuddered and gasped for air between the violent, uncontrollable sobs that wracked my body. Slowly, as if emerging from a thick fog, my mind began to process reality. It was Emerson's comforting presence surrounding me, not the vile specter of Maurice. Maurice was dead, his wretched existence forever extinguished...and yet, his malevolent ghost still lurked in the shadows of my psyche, an insidious phantom that refused to release its grip on my tortured memories.

"I'm sorry, I'm sorry, I'm sorry," I sobbed, crumpling against Emerson's chest.

His arms wrapped around my back, soothing caresses over my hair. "Shh, it's all right honey, you have nothing to apologize for; I'm not upset. Just breathe for me."

Focusing on Emerson's soothing words, I drew in a deep, shuddering breath, followed by another and another, until the well of tears gradually ran dry. With trembling arms, I pushed myself up, blinking away the lingering moisture from my eyes. As my vision cleared, my gaze drifted over the expanse of his bare chest, and a fresh wave of guilt washed over me at the sight of the deep, angry gouges marring his skin—wounds inflicted by my own hands in the throes of my waking nightmare.

"Emerson!" I gasped, immediately moving off him and kneeling at his side. "I'm so sorry. I...I don't know what happened."

"It's all right, Aurelia. I shouldn't have been above you, made you feel trapped. I'm the one that's sorry."

Fresh tears poured down my cheeks, dripping off my jaw to land on his bare skin. Gesturing disgustedly at the wounds I'd wrought, I said, "How can I possibly be your mate? You were so gentle and loving, and I did this. I never should have called out to you. Leave me, Emerson. Just leave. You'll never be safe with me."

With that, I sank back onto the bed, my body trembling with the force of my sobs. I rubbed at my eyes with the heels of my hands, trying in vain to stem the flow of tears. My legs curled up instinctively, and I began rocking back and forth as I continued to cry, my breath coming in ragged gasps. Soft hands brushed against my wrists, gently easing them away from my face. I resisted at first, not wanting to see the damage I had wrought, but eventually I allowed him to pull my hands away. My eyes came up slowly to meet Emerson's, anguish plain on my face. I expected to see anger, disappointment, even fear in his gaze. But I found no trace of blame or recrimination. Only love shone from those emerald depths, a love so pure and unconditional that it took my breath away.

"You are my mate, Aurelia, and we will figure this out together. If you can't handle something, next time, we'll try something else. All right? But I'm not leaving you. Ever. You are mine, as I am yours."

His words were finally breaking through, the utter sincerity in his voice unmistakable. It gave me the strength I needed to suck in another breath.

"I freaking love you," I said, tears still dripping from my lashes. It was the first time I'd said it aloud, though I'd known it longer than I cared to admit.

Emerson's smile dazzled me. His voice sounded tight with emotion when he responded. "I freaking love you, too, woman."

Leaning forward to close the few inches of space between us, I pressed my lips against his once, not ready to allow it to go any further yet but needing the contact. Releasing him, my gaze dropped back to the angry red lines across his chest. Looking around the room, my gaze landed on a healing cream I'd put together and used after battles.

"Lay down," I ordered, scrambling over to the small jar and bringing it back to the bed with me. Unscrewing the lid, I dipped two fingers inside and placed the soothing balm over the worst of the wounds. He hissed out a breath, and I winced. "Sorry, it'll sting a bit, but then it'll help."

"It's fine; it was just a shock at first," he said with a forced smile, putting on his manliest face.

Giving him a half-smile of my own, I continued to apply the ointment until every scratch had been covered. His blood already worked to heal the cuts, closing them over in the Elemental way, but the cream would speed this along.

When I finished with the jar, I set it aside but allowed my eyes to trail along his nude form. He lay perfectly still, seeming to understand my need even if I didn't. My fingers traced each wound lightly, then continued to follow each chiseled muscle against his flat stomach.

His breath hitched the lower I went, and I watched his expression carefully to make sure I wouldn't hurt him. I would do everything in my power to never hurt him again. *Quite the opposite. It feels very good. I'm not hiding that fact from you, but please don't think I expect anything.*

Knowing he spoke the truth, I nodded and continued my slow perusal. He had been the first man I'd ever had an attraction to, and I wanted to explore, even if it couldn't go any further.

Once I finished tracing with my fingertips, I leaned forward with a tentative lick along the worst of the wounds. Emerson sucked in a breath as his stomach tightened, and I found myself enjoying his reaction. Emboldened, I continued the slow assault, opening my mind to his so I could feel what he felt.

Immeasurable pleasure, built from a kind of teasing torture, nearly overwhelmed me. It felt similar to what I had experienced when he'd built me up, before the amazing release. My hands and mouth continued to explore, finding every nook and nuance that made Emerson gasp. Every time I found one, I explored further, eager to hear that little noise from the back of his throat again.

Oddly, though his hands remained at his sides and he kept perfectly still, I felt my own body winding up with his. His pleasure fed my own, and from being in his mind, I knew the opposite to be true, also.

Understanding this, I felt confident to take the next step. I knelt above him, sucking in a deep breath. Swinging one leg over his until I straddled his hips, I waited, testing myself. Emerson's hands smoothed across my thigh, slow and gentle, not gripping but letting me know whatever choice I made would be all right with him.

Our eyes locked, and I let out a breath as I lowered over him, the feeling of being joined together nearly overwhelming. I paused there, allowing the sensations to wash through me before I began to move. Emerson's hands remained gentle as they slid over my thighs, up to my waist, and lit my nerve endings as he continued to softly explore. That wonderful release built again, slow and steady.

You are so incredibly beautiful, Emerson's husky voice only added to the blazing fire that slowly consumed me. *Do you feel how perfectly we fit together? You were made for me, Aurelia, and I for you.*

My gaze steady on his, I gripped his hands with my own and held on tight. *This is okay?*

This is perfect.

More confident now, I kept up my pace, my mind open to his. My own pleasure fed his, as his did mine. There were no secrets between us, no hidden agenda. We were one body, one soul, moving toward the inevitable fall. I felt it low in my stomach, building and winding tight.

"Emerson," I whispered, his name my solace.

"Let go, Aurelia. I'll catch you." The tidal wave began again, threatening to carry me away. In response, I gripped Emerson tighter, knowing he would hold me to the earth when I felt like I would float up to the stars. *That's it, let go for me. Know what it can be like between us. Give yourself into my keeping.*

His whispered words shattered the last of my restraint, and I cried out, my body convulsing with ecstasy as I came undone in his arms. The force of my climax triggered his own release, and he let out a hoarse, guttural cry that was the sweetest music to my ears. We clung to each other, riding out the waves of pleasure that crashed over us, lost in a sea of sensation. In that moment, nothing else existed but the two of us, our bodies and souls entwined as one.

Chapter 16

We lay entwined for a long time after I collapsed against his chest, our hearts beating as one and gradually slowing to a steadier rhythm. The silence between us was comfortable and content, with no need for words. Emerson's mind remained open to mine, as mine did to his, our thoughts and feelings flowing freely between us. It was a moment of pure bliss and tranquility, a perfect snapshot of happiness that made all the years of pain and struggle worth enduring. In that singular instant, everything else faded away until only the two of us existed, lost in the profound connection we shared.

I didn't want to break our perfect embrace, but something important needed to be said. Lifting my head off his chest, I met his gaze head-on with no fear. He watched me, relaxed and seeming content to remain as we were.

"I love you," I told him again, needing to say the words. "I never thought I would have anything like this. I never thought I would live through the confrontation with Maurice, but you not only helped me achieve that, you've given me so much more. You've given me a life worth living."

His eyes softened even more, drinking me in. "Aurelia, I would give you the whole world. I love you more than my own life."

With a light touch, he brushed his thumb along my cheek as if memorizing each curve of my face. I lowered enough to press my lips against his, my body instantly coming alive. I could feel Emerson do the same through our physical connection and our mental one.

"I had no idea it could be like this."

Brushing my hair away from my face, Emerson replied, "How could you? In truth, I didn't know either. We were told as children the connection between mates, but words alone couldn't do this justice."

"All my experience comes from pain and terror," I admitted in a low voice. "I want you to replace every one of those memories with what lovemaking should be."

Emerson grinned, his eyes lighting with love. "Anything for my mate."

As the night wore on, Emerson and I lost ourselves in the intimate exploration of each other's bodies, discovering the places that sparked desire and pushed the boundaries of ecstasy. With each tender caress and passionate kiss, he carefully navigated my limits, his patience and understanding never wavering. In his arms, I found a safe haven where my confidence as a woman could flourish, nurtured by his unwavering love and acceptance.

Though the shadows of my past might forever prevent me from surrendering to the vulnerability of being beneath him, Emerson's reassuring words and gentle touch made it abundantly clear that it held no bearing on his devotion. In the sacred space we created together, there existed an infinite array of ways to express our love and indulge in the pleasures of our union, each one a testament to the unbreakable bond we shared. With every breath and every sigh, I felt the shackles of my fears begin to crumble, replaced by an all-consuming sense of freedom and belonging.

I could feel his hunger beating at him, his need to taste my blood and make me wholly his. It was the one thing we didn't share—couldn't share.

Emerson couldn't drink from me; I wouldn't allow it. His presence lessened my pain, but it still made itself known, always lurking around the corner. Even with our joining, my soul still remained shadowed, my blood still tainted.

"Are you sure you're comfortable with meeting Reya, Jade, and Kate?" Emerson asked casually as the sun reached its apex.

Our limbs remained entangled as we reclined on the bed, our bodies intertwined in a lovers' embrace. The sun's harsh rays filtering through the curtains served as a reminder of my inability to venture outdoors during these daylight hours, but that fact appeared to be of no concern to him. He seemed content to simply bask in our closeness, his fingers tracing idle patterns on my skin as we lay together. I responded to his query with sincerity, my voice soft but unwavering.

"I don't know. But if I don't, then Edith definitely won't. Anya might still—she may be the bravest of us all."

"I understand," Emerson said, and I knew he truly did. "I will be with you no matter what you decide. And I will support anything Edith or Anya decides, as well. Dominic and I both already see them as family. Sisters we never had."

"Thank you," I said, feeling a weight lift off me. I knew how important this was to Emerson—how important it could be to me. It didn't change the fact that I felt terrified. Then, I remembered something else about this cave, something that we'd been a little too distracted to enjoy. Standing abruptly, I took Emerson's hand and hauled him to his feet. "Come with me."

He laughed and followed as I marched to the back of the cave, finding another small crack in the stone. I quickly dissolved into mist to get through, with Emerson close behind. After moving a few feet through seemingly solid stone, another small room opened up.

Inside sat a deep pool of water, its surface still and mirror-like, reflecting the dim light that filtered into the small chamber. The water was ice cold, a stark contrast to the warmth of the cave beyond. I reformed along the edge, my body materializing from the misty tendrils that had carried me through the narrow crack in the stone. Without hesitation, I knelt down, the rough rock digging into my knees as I placed my palms flat against the surface of the pool. Murmuring an incantation, I focused my energy on the water, feeling the power of the words flow through me and into the depths below.

Slowly, the chill began to recede, replaced by a growing warmth that emanated from my hands. Though this pool was fed by an underground spring that ran deep beneath the earth before emptying into the lake outside, I knew from experience that my magic would keep the water hot for a good hour, providing a perfect respite.

"This is amazing," Emerson said with appreciation.

Stepping down into the pool, I waited for Emerson to join me before sinking all the way in, submerging my body in the soothing warmth. I dunked my head beneath the surface, feeling the water caress my scalp as my hair fanned out around me like a golden halo. In the corner, a basket of shampoo and soap that I'd left in here still remained, untouched and pristine, as if waiting patiently for my return after all the years I'd been away. The familiar scents of lavender and vanilla wafted through the steamy air, evoking memories of countless hours spent luxuriating in this very spot.

"Allow me," Emerson said, reaching into the basket to lather the shampoo between his palms.

I straddled his lap as he massaged it into my hair, feeling more relaxed than I could ever remember. His soothing, gentle fingers worked their magic on my scalp. The combination of hot water and bare skin left me achy and needy all over again.

"Seriously, will it ever be enough?" I asked, dipping my head back to rinse out the shampoo. "Now that I know how good this part can be, I can't seem to get enough."

Emerson chuckled huskily, picking up the bar of soap next. "I hope it's never enough. I could spend a decade alone in this cave with you and not miss the outside world for a moment."

"Not even your brother?" I asked, my eyebrow raised.

"We can speak telepathically," he said with a deceptively casual shrug.

"What about your nieces? Won't you want to meet them?"

"All right, you got me." He grinned and began rubbing the soap along my skin. "I'm going to spoil them rotten."

"I had a feeling. You'll also be overprotective, and you'll try to be stern, but I have a feeling you're going to be a big pushover."

"Don't tell Dominic."

Laughing, I took the soap and ran it over his broad shoulders, my eyes lingering there. My voice soft, I asked, "Do you want children of your own?"

He stilled completely, his intense gaze fixed intently on my face as he waited for me to meet his eyes. The silence stretched between us, heavy and charged with unspoken emotions. I tried to resist the magnetic pull of his stare, but finally, unable to bear the weighted quiet any longer, I lifted my head and looked directly into his emerald eyes. "I would love to have children with you, but only if and when you're ready. And if you're never ready, I will enjoy every moment we have together."

The minor terror I'd been feeling at being rejected suddenly cleared, and I leaned forward to press my lips against his. I poured all my thoughts and feelings into the kiss, needing to tell him how I felt but not having the words.

He gripped my hips firmly as I rose above him, my body trembling with anticipation. Slowly, I lowered myself down, joining us together as true mates should be, our bodies becoming one. Moving with a languid, sensual rhythm, the water created an intriguing buoyancy effect, heightening every sensation. On a soft, breathy sigh, I took the leap, surrendering myself completely to the moment and to him. Emerson's strong arms wrapped securely around my back, holding me close against his chest as he followed me over the edge, our pleasure intertwining. We remained as we were, basking in the afterglow, our hearts beating in perfect harmony, the warm, soothing water lulling me into the sweet promise of contented sleep in his loving embrace.

We rose together, floating above the water, through the crack in the wall, and back to the mattress of soft feathers. Settling into Emerson's side, I allowed my eyes to drift closed as the sun made its arc across the sky. I felt thoroughly satisfied, at least for the moment, and deliciously sore. Now, I just wanted to lay here beside Emerson as we waited out the sun. "Tell me more about your childhood."

Emerson's low, husky voice whispered into my ear, reminding me of all the days he spoke into my mind. That was how he'd won me over, how I'd fallen irreversibly in love with him.

The next few days felt like pure heaven. As Emerson had said, we easily could have spent years in the little cave without another soul interrupting us. But, by mutual agreement, we decided to return to our family. We had a duty to Edith and Anya, not to mention Dominic, Reese, and their unborn children. I dressed in my most comfortable clothes—black leather pants and jacket, with my trusty weapons belt around my hips. I'd already moved all the items I wanted to keep into the bags we'd brought, and Emerson lifted them easily with one hand.

"Are you ready?" he asked quietly, knowing my mixed feelings on leaving this place.

Taking one last look around the small cave that had been my home, I nodded and took his offered hand. "I'm ready."

The only thing I wasn't taking with me was the mattress, but it had been made from natural materials, and I gifted it back to the earth, thanking her for providing for me when I needed it. All spell traces were erased, releasing the cave back to the wild and any who explored this far.

We headed down the hill, content to hike at a human pace. The setting sun reflected stunning oranges and reds across the lake, and we took a moment to watch the beauty of nature.

"I know you went through a trying time here, but I will always look fondly on this place," Emerson said quietly.

Nudging him with my shoulder, I kept my sarcastic reply in check and answered him truthfully. "Thanks to you, I will too. Maybe one day...a few years from now...we could come back."

"Whenever you're ready," Emerson promised.

We turned then, hand in hand, and made our way toward civilization. Once we were away from the lake, we upped our speed to a run, as it was easier than trying to carry all of the bags in a different form.

Is Jace still around?

He is.

I would like to meet with him. I think I can handle it now.

Emerson squeezed my hand. *If at any point you need to leave, we will leave.*

Knowing I had Emerson's unwavering support and love meant everything to me. His presence alone gave me the strength and courage I needed to face whatever lay ahead. We arrived at the hotel, the bustling lobby a stark contrast to the serene tranquility of the lake we had just left behind. Dominic, ever the thoughtful brother, had already reserved a room for us, and we quickly deposited my meager belongings there. Jace had his own accommodations, so we made our way to his room before I could change my mind. As we approached his door, I took a deep, steadying breath, bracing myself for his appearance and the flood of emotions it might unleash. I silently reminded myself that Maurice no longer held any power or control over my life. He was a ghost of the past, and I refused to let him haunt my present or future any longer.

"Emerson, Arie, welcome," Jace said, moving aside to allow us entry. "Thank you for coming to see me. I apologize for frightening you."

"It's nothing you did," I assured him.

"Dominic explained a bit about your past; I hope you don't mind. I'm a healer, Arie, and I've also worked as a doctor for humans over the years. I understand trauma. Rest assured, I take no offense."

Nodding, I sucked in a deep breath. "Would you examine me? Anya said you were able to lessen her pain."

"I was, but I fear it was only a Band-Aid. Reese's idea of Reya and the other talented women working with you seems like your best shot, long-term." Jace motioned for me to get comfortable, and I moved without lessening my death grip on Emerson's hand. Though he spoke soothingly into my mind, my pulse still thrummed with nerves. "I'm going to connect my spirit to yours. You'll feel a warmth traveling through you. Try to relax."

"I'm ready." Jace sat beside me, his eyes closing as he concentrated. Not having to look at the provoking irises helped me to settle. As he'd warned, I felt strange heat traveling through my body. Occasionally, I'd squeeze Emerson's hand; otherwise, we remained silent. Several minutes passed, then several more. Still, Jace didn't move. A gnawing in the pit of my stomach told me something had gone wrong. "Emerson, we need to wake him up."

"How do I even do that?"

"I don't know, but we need to try." In a flash, Emerson crouched before the healer, grabbing his upper arms and calling his name urgently. Jace remained unresponsive, his eyes closed and his body limp. Dominic appeared moments later, his brow furrowed with concern, but he had no more insight on how to snap Jace out of the strange stupor he'd fallen into. Panic began to set in, doubling when Edith arrived in the room, her eyes wide with fear as she took in the scene before her. The tension in the air was palpable as Edith walked determinedly toward the healer. "No! You have to get out of here, Edith. Something is wrong."

"Let me try," she said with utter calm. Emerson and Dominic backed away uncertainly, but Edith paid them no mind. She reached out and took Jace's hand in hers, eyes slipping closed as she made the connection.

We all watched for a tense few minutes until I simultaneously felt Jace's heat leave my body, and both their eyes blinked open. Relief rushed through me. "What just happened?"

Jace stared at Edith in awe; she met his gaze head-on, though I could hear her quickened heartbeat from here. For a pregnant moment, it seemed as if the two forgot we existed. Finally breaking the connection, Edith stepped away from Jace and looked at me. "Maurice's blood had him trapped. I was able to connect with him and guide him out."

I looked over to Jace—he seemed shaken to his core. Something more had happened here. *Emerson?*

Yes. I believe they're mates.

Chapter 17

Everyone in the room stared at Edith in shock, their eyes wide and mouths agape. The air was thick with tension as the weight of her words settled over them. She was clearly uncomfortable with the attention, her shoulders hunched and her hands clasped tightly in front of her, but she held her head high, a picture of defiance even while refusing to meet Jace's intense gaze. His shock blue eyes bore into her, searching for answers, but she kept hers averted. "I would like to go back to my room now," she said, her voice steady despite the tremor of emotion that ran through it. Without waiting for a response, she turned on her heel and strode out of the room, her long black hair swaying behind her.

Dominic acted quickly. "I will escort her back."

They left without a backward glance at Jace. Stunned, my mouth worked, but no sound came out. Thankfully, Emerson understood and took over. "Are you all right? Do you need blood?"

"No, no, I'm fine, though I'm a bit tired. Would you mind terribly if I rested for a while?"

"Of course," Emerson said, guiding me to my feet.

"I'm sorry that I wasn't able to help you," Jace added before we left. "I had hoped to at least lessen your pain."

"It's all right. I'm used to it."

"Whatever it takes, Arie. For you, Anya—and Edith. We'll figure out a way to eradicate the shadow of evil from your lives."

"Thank you. Rest now; we'll check on you tomorrow evening."

We left Jace's room and headed directly for Edith and Anya's quarters, our footsteps echoing through the dimly lit hallway. Worry etched on their faces, Reese, Dominic, and Anya met us halfway, their eyes flickering between Emerson and me. Reese glanced toward Edith's closed door, a slight frown tugging at her lips, before explaining in a hushed tone, "She'd like to be alone for a while."

"She's okay?"

"She will be. Why don't we all get some dinner?"

I understood the unspoken reasoning behind Reese's request. We needed somewhere more private to speak. "Let's go."

Walking with Anya wedged protectively between us, Dominic led us to a restaurant a few blocks away and asked for a private dining area. The host led us behind a curtain and into a secluded room, where we settled around a worn wooden table.

Walking with Anya wedged protectively between us, Dominic led us to a restaurant a few blocks away and asked for a private dining area. The host, sensing the urgency in Dominic's voice, quickly obliged and led us behind a heavy velvet curtain into a secluded room. The space was dimly lit, with a few flickering candles casting a warm glow on the worn wooden table that dominated the center of the room. We settled around it, the chairs creaking slightly beneath our weight.

By mutual agreement, we let Anya do the ordering. Her Russian accent seemed to thicken as she spoke to the waiter in her native tongue, the words flowing effortlessly from her lips. In only a few minutes, we each received a steaming bowl of borscht, the rich aroma of the hearty soup filling the air. A basket of freshly baked rye bread accompanied the meal, the crust a perfect golden brown. Anya broke off a chunk, the bread still warm to the touch, even as she turned her soft blue eyes to us and asked, "What's happened with Edith?"

I explained my time with Jace and how Edith came to the rescue. Dominic and Reese seemed to understand the implications, and Anya didn't take long to add two and two.

"Are they mates?"

"We think so. Tell us about what's been happening since we've been gone." Emerson and I had traveled separately with Edith and Anya to get to this town since Edith hadn't wanted to interact with Jace. They must not have met in the time since, either.

"Jace understood Edith's hesitation to be examined. He's been keeping an eye on the babies every evening, but he's kept to himself otherwise." Reese took a spoonful of soup and sighed. "This is really good, but man, what I wouldn't give for a greasy slice of pizza."

Dominic chuckled. I didn't know that I'd heard him laugh before. "Our first stop back in the States, I promise."

Seeming satisfied by that, Reese continued, "We've gone out with Anya each night to practice her abilities, but Edith has remained behind. She hasn't said so, but I think the wide-open spaces frighten her a bit."

"She was held underground for so long. Even when Maurice traveled from place to place, he would drug her—us—and keep us in cages."

Anya nodded. "Edith likes to have the window open all day and night. She really likes the bath. And people watching—but from the safety of our room. She just needs time."

"We'll give her all the time she needs. Jace needs to do the same."

"I think he's aware of her delicate situation," Dominic said. "But I will speak with him to put your minds at ease."

"Edith has all of us for protection." Emerson squeezed my hand, and I met his gaze lovingly. If Jace had half the patience of my mate, Edith would be just fine. In fact, I wanted this for her. For Anya, too. We all deserved to be happy.

But first, she had to live on her own, to truly discover who she was now that she no longer answered to Maurice's tyranny. She needed the time and space to find herself, to heal from the trauma of her past, and build a new life free from fear and oppression. No matter what it took, I would make sure she could do just that. I would support her every step of the way, providing the love, encouragement, and resources she needed to thrive. Her happiness and well-being were my top priorities, and I was determined to see her through this journey of self-discovery and empowerment.

When we arrived back at the hotel, Anya brought extra food she'd ordered for Edith up to their shared room. Though I wanted to go with, see Edith for myself, Anya convinced me to let her handle it. After I made her promise to update me as soon as possible, Emerson and I followed Dominic and Reese back to their room.

Reese sat in a chair and propped her feet up on the bed while Dominic showed us our travel documents. "The closest airport is Magadan. We can get to Moscow from there, then on to New York."

"You're thinking Minneapolis after that, then Duluth?"

Dominic nodded. "We can stay on my property there for now. Jade and Talon offered any of us places to stay in Sun Valley, as well."

"Edith, Anya, and I don't care as long as we get out of Russia. Out of Europe, altogether."

Emerson squeezed my hand. "As long as we all stay together."

"We should talk to Jace about this, too," Reese said. "Things might be different for him now."

"He'd be welcome, as long as Edith feels comfortable with that," Dominic said. "We have a few days before our flight; hopefully they can come to agreeable terms before then."

"Jace is coming for the wedding either way, right?" Reese asked.

"He indicated as much."

"One of us will be at Edith's side at all times," Reese continued. "I just wish she would come out and train with us. Her gift is extremely powerful, but she needs training on the basic stuff."

"I will speak with her," I said. "If I ask, she'll do her best to join Anya's sessions."

Reese nodded. "I'm still learning, too. This is all pretty new for me."

"Actually, Arie, we were hoping you might show us all some things," Dominic said.

Startled, I looked between them. Emerson nearly glowed with pride. "Me?"

"You and possibly Jace. He's been around longer, but you're able to do things I didn't know were possible."

"That's because I learned from shadowmen. I learned from the darkness."

Reese and Dominic exchanged a look before Dominic shrugged. "Magic and power are neither good nor bad, light nor dark. That comes from how you use it."

"All right," I said, knowing he spoke the truth. "I will show you what I know."

We all were surprised by the knock on the door. Dominic answered, genuine pleasure in his voice when he found Anya and Edith both on the other side. Edith stepped into the room with her head held high, apology in her eyes. "I know you are all concerned about me, so I wanted to say that I am fine. This world will take some adjusting for me, and I will admit that I have been afraid. That stops now."

Stepping to the woman I considered my sister, I took her hands and said, "You take all the time you need."

"Am I not the one who spoke of the wonders of the world? Encouraged you to escape so you could experience them again? It is time for me to do the same."

"That's wonderful news."

She gave my hands a squeeze before releasing them. "I would also like to address the obvious bond between Jace and myself. While I acknowledge that there is a connection between us, I do not yet know what to do about it. He has respected my wishes thus far, and I believe he will continue to do so. He is a good man; this much I saw from our contact earlier. Whatever happens next will be between us."

"We support whatever decisions you make," I said. Everyone else in the room nodded in agreement. "Speaking of, we were just discussing travel plans. We will first fly to Moscow, then to the States. Jace will be coming with us. Is that all right with you?"

"Yes, that is fine."

"Anya, you'll be all right traveling through Moscow?"

She raised her head high. "We are not staying? Just stopping on our way?"

I nodded. "Just stopping. We won't leave the airport."

"Then I'm fine. Let us leave this country of my birth. It is time."

"We have a few days, but then we'll do just that. For tonight, why don't we get some practice in? Edith, are you ready?"

She sucked in a breath and steeled herself for facing the outside. "I am."

We ventured out together, our images blurring and distorting as we reached the outskirts of town and plunged into the abandoned forests that lay beyond. I searched for a spot sheltered by a dense canopy of trees, hoping that the dappled shade and comforting presence of nature would ease Edith's transition as she emerged from her subterranean existence. The lush foliage seemed to whisper words of encouragement, and the gentle rustle of leaves in the breeze promised a new beginning. I wanted to make this first foray into the outside world as gentle and nurturing as possible for Edith, knowing the enormous adjustment she faced after so long underground.

Throughout the night, I showed them basic spells and had them practicing as if we were in school. Edith had retained as much, if not more, knowledge as I had from her captivity. The only difference was she'd never had an opportunity to try it for herself.

On the second night, Jace joined us. He shared his knowledge and learned from me in return. Though he specialized in healing, he'd spent time exploring the wide range of abilities he possessed as an Elemental. The men and I worked with Edith, Anya, and Reese at shifting into other animal forms. Reese had had little time to practice but was able to transform into a wolf at will. Edith had some trouble shifting back into her natural form, landing on her butt even as I made sure to clothe her.

She let out a surprised huff of air when she found herself on the ground. Jace offered a hand to help her up, which she stared at for a long time. When she finally accepted his offer, I could practically see the electricity flowing between them.

On our third night, the last before we made the trek into Magadan, Emerson and I stopped in town so he could fill up on blood. The others went ahead without us—Dominic had been making sure the other three women were fed daily—and we walked hand in hand. For a little while, I could pretend we were on a date, living normal lives. I wondered if this is what it would be like in the States.

"It could be."

"You need to stop walking around my mind. You never know what you'll find in there."

I like when you think about me. When you replay our alone time or ponder what we should do during our next alone time... His husky words instantly turned me to mush. Fire sizzled along my veins and pooled low in my stomach. The alley next to us seemed dark enough. We could just blur our image. Emerson could hold me up against the wall while I wrapped my legs around his waist.... *Damnit, woman. You'll be the death of me.*

Satisfaction rolled from me in waves. That, and a sharp need that wouldn't be assuaged. *When we get to the States, I think we will need a week or two alone.*

He brought my hand to his mouth and nibbled along my knuckles. *You'll have no complaint from me.*

We found a handful of men for Emerson to feed from, then made our way to the outskirts of town. As we neared the clearing where we were to meet the others, I felt, more than heard, a sudden jarring note reverberating through the earth. Emerson and I both paused, instantly on alert. Through our connection, I could feel him reaching out to his brother, and I heard the echo of Dominic's short reply.

Shadowmen.

Without a word between us, Emerson and I began to run, following the direction in the earth, real panic making my heart pound. I'd left them alone, unprotected. I couldn't live with myself if something happened to Reese and her babies. To Edith or Anya. I would never allow them to become prisoners again.

As we approached the small clearing, Emerson and I decelerated, our steps becoming more cautious and deliberate. We needed to assess the situation, to understand the threat we faced. In the center of the glade, four shadowmen stood in a menacing formation, their dark forms a stark contrast to the vibrant greens of the surrounding forest. They faced off against Dominic and Jace, who stood protectively in front of the women, shielding them with their own bodies. The air crackled with tension, the impending battle hanging heavy in the atmosphere. But even as I focused on the immediate danger, I could sense another presence lurking in the shadows, biding its time, waiting for the perfect moment to strike.

You feel him? I sent to Emerson.

To the north, he confirmed. *I'll circle around; you go help Dominic.*

Nodding, I flicked my knives into my palms and stalked forward. Clouds had gathered, lightning arcing across the sky. Edith and Anya had gathered Reese between them in defensive positions while she wielded the ultimate form of electricity.

Dominic engaged two of the shadowmen in a fierce battle, his movements swift and precise as he parried their attacks. Nearby, Jace held his own against the other two, his elemental powers crackling through the air. Reese's lightning strikes illuminated the scene in flashes of brilliant white, keeping the creatures constantly on the move. They flowed from one place to another, trying to evade her electrifying assaults, their shadowy forms twisting and contorting in an eerie dance.

One of the shadowmen disappeared from a lightning strike, only to reappear beside Anya, spurring me into motion. I trusted Reese not to strike me down as I moved like a blur across the ground, sending out my knives ahead of my fists.

It caught the shadowman by surprise, one poisoned knife sticking from his chest as the second whizzed past his neck, barely missing as he turned. The poison would move quickly, but I had to make sure he remained immobile before I could focus on the second shadowman, still dancing with Reese's lightning and Jace's attacks.

Mother Earth, strong and true. Twist and bind, make unbreakable vines. Halt this man's attack; this I ask of you. Roots and leaves, spare twigs and bramble joined together and formed ropes, wrapping around the shadowman tight. Knowing he wouldn't be a problem, I called out to Anya. "Fire! They need to burn!"

Trusting in her newfound powers, I spun and brought two more weapons into my hands. This next shadowman was a wily one, easily avoiding each strike as it slammed into the ground. I studied his movements for a moment and aimed my first knife for his next step. It slammed home, hitting him high in the right shoulder.

Using his surprise to launch forward, I took him to the ground with a scissor kick, falling with him and immediately rolling out of the way as Reese shot lightning into his prone form. The shadowman lit up like a Christmas tree, his unnerving shrieks mixing with the first as their noxious scent clogged my nose.

Springing to my feet, I took off at a run to help Dominic and Jace, who had teamed up against the remaining two but were unable to get the upper hand. With a flick of my wrist, one knife lodged into the shadowman's back closest to me.

He roared with rage and spun to attack, but I was ready. Easily evading his initial strikes, I began to return my own, my movements fluid and precise. I jerked to a halt when searing pain knocked the breath from my lungs, causing me to gasp and sink to the ground. My brain desperately tried to ascertain what had happened, searching for the source of the agony that now consumed me. When I heard Emerson's panicked voice, his words simultaneously sent to Dominic and me through our mental link, the urgency in his tone sent a chill down my spine, and I struggled to push myself back to my feet, knowing that we had to prepare for the imminent threat. *He's coming!*

The pain abruptly shut off, and I pushed myself to all fours, sucking in a breath as I realized what had happened. Emerson and I were so closely connected that I had felt his pain. I felt tears spring to my eyes as I realized Emerson had been gravely wounded, but I snapped back to the moment as I heard my name cried out above the melee. "Arie, watch out!"

Edith's desperate cry pierced through the chaos. I grappled with the shadowman, trying to push him off, but his weight bore down on me relentlessly. Punch after brutal punch rained upon my body, each blow sending shockwaves of agony through my ribs and face. I thrashed beneath him, my struggles growing weaker with each passing second. Darkness crept in at the edges of my vision, threatening to pull me under. I clung to consciousness, refusing to succumb. I couldn't die, not now, not when I had just begun to truly live, to love, to find purpose.

Pinned to the unyielding earth, I remained trapped while the dark figure relentlessly attacked me. His fists pummeled my body in a merciless barrage, each blow more vicious than the last. I gasped for breath, my lungs burning as I struggled against his crushing weight. The ground beneath me felt like an unforgiving prison, offering no escape from the onslaught of violence. Desperation clawed at my heart as I realized the gravity of my situation, my strength waning with every passing second. The shadowy assailant seemed to draw power from my growing weakness, his assault intensifying in its brutality. With my remaining strength I sent my spirit seeking help in the earth. *Mother Earth, strong and true...*

Another blow to the head disrupted my thoughts. I had arrived at the end of my strength, my focus gone. *Mother Earth...*

Through the haze and ringing in my ears, a noise came through loud and clear. A vengeful shriek, a battle cry. In a moment, the assault came to an end, and I lay in a bloody and broken heap. In the next second, Edith's face hovered above mine, blood-splattered and frightened. "Arie? Arie, can you hear me?"

Her voice came from a great distance, muffled and distorted as if she were calling to me from underwater. My eyes, nearly swollen shut from the brutal beating, strained to focus on her face hovering above mine. Through the haze of pain and the ringing in my ears, I struggled to concentrate. There was something important, something crucial I needed to do, but the thought slipped away like wisps of smoke, lost in the fog of my battered mind. I fought to hold onto consciousness, knowing that if I succumbed to the darkness, I might never find my way back.

"I need...sit up," I forced through my raw throat.

When I attempted this on my own, Edith wrapped her arms around me for support. Four shadowmen lay dead in the clearing, but there was still one more. Dominic faced off with the one who had been hiding, but Emerson was nowhere to be found. Jace looked torn between seeing to Edith and helping Dominic. Edith wrapped her arms around me and called out to Jace. "Help him!"

No...

Emerson! I screamed through our link. There was no response. I couldn't even feel him. *No! Emerson!* I cried again, unable to handle even the idea of his loss. It couldn't be true. I loved him. I needed him.

I must have been babbling aloud, for Edith began soothing me, whispering nonsense that didn't quite break through the fog.

"Emerson," I croaked, then forced my eyes open again.

Jace charged fearlessly into the fray, determined to aid his comrades, but a potent blast of arcane energy slammed into him, sending him reeling backward. Edith's scream pierced the air, her anguish palpable as she witnessed her mate's plight. Dominic, battered and weary from his relentless battle against the shadowmen, stood his ground defiantly, unwilling to yield despite the toll the fight had taken on him. Reese, her face etched with stark terror, unleashed bolts of lightning that crackled and danced around the powerful adversary, yet they seemed to dissipate harmlessly against an invisible barrier. Anya, in a desperate attempt to harness the earth's power, knelt with her hands plunged into the soil, her fingers clawing at the ground as she sought to summon the strength she needed. But even her valiant efforts appeared insufficient against the overwhelming might of their foe.

I had to help them. My family. "Stand."

"What?" Edith tore her gaze from Jace—barely moving but alive—to look at me. "Arie, no, you are injured."

I tried to shake my head, but it pounded in response. "Stand."

Against her better judgment, Edith helped me to my feet. Though I leaned heavily on her, I managed to stay upright. "Knives," I whispered, clumsily grasping one with my left hand. The right had been crushed and hung useless at my side.

Edith took one in her free hand, determination set on her face. I was proud of her at that moment—not only had she rescued me just now, but she was prepared to fight for Dominic and Jace. And if Emerson was truly gone, I didn't have much to live for. I'd make certain my death meant life for those remaining.

Jace struggled to his feet as I hobbled closer to the ensuing fight. He moved to stop us, but I gathered all my remaining strength, borrowing from the earth itself, and launched the poisoned knife. Edith followed suit, and they stuck in the remaining shadowman's back, one after the other.

The shadowman let out an ear-piercing shriek of pure rage as he fell to his knees, his dark form crumpling under the weight of our relentless assault. Dominic stood above him, his chest heaving with each labored breath, his body bruised and bloody from the intense battle. Despite his battered state, Dominic gathered his remaining strength, preparing himself for the final, decisive attack. Two large vines erupted from the earth beneath the shadowman, their thorny tendrils wrapping around his limbs and digging into his inky skin, holding him in place and rendering him immobile.

My attention diverted from the scene as a figure tumbled out from the thick foliage of the surrounding trees. Blood streaked down from a gash on his temple, and a huge, gaping wound marred his chest. For a moment, my heart plummeted, fearing the worst, but then it leaped with a surge of relief as I realized it was Emerson, and he was still alive. His emerald eyes met mine, and the anguish I saw within their depths nearly tore me apart. I reached out to him through our mental link, desperate to connect with him, to share in his pain and offer what comfort I could. But to my surprise and dismay, I found myself shut out, unable to access his thoughts or emotions. Somehow, despite his grave injuries, Emerson had managed to close himself off from me, refusing to let me bear witness to the extent of his suffering.

"I'm sorry," he whispered across the clearing, though I could hear him clear as day. When someone was lodged into your very soul, distance hardly mattered. Dominic reached his brother and supported his weight, leading him back to the struggling shadowman. He was a powerful one; though we had outnumbered these evil creatures, we all had taken a beating.

The brothers faced the shadowman with livid expressions. There was something more going on here—something that my brain couldn't connect through the haze. When Dominic spoke, he had an odd sort of calm in his tone. "You killed our parents. You attempted to take my mate from me. My family. Today, you meet your fate."

The shadowman snarled viciously as Dominic held out his hand, palm up, a look of fierce determination etched upon his face. Emerson placed his own palm beneath his brother's, linking their power together in a display of unbreakable unity. Together, they summoned a fireball, its flames licking the air with an intense heat, and immediately launched it into the evil abomination before them.

This was the very creature they'd been hunting relentlessly since the day they'd discovered their parents' bodies, their lives forever changed by the heinous act of violence that had torn their family apart.

The shadowman's body ignited with the supernatural fire, his agonized shriek piercing the night air and echoing through the surrounding landscape. Dominic and Emerson watched with a grim sort of satisfaction as their enemy burned to a crisp, the flames consuming his form until nothing remained but ashes scattered in the wind. I felt an overwhelming sense of pride for my mate; his strength and power astounded me, leaving me in awe of the incredible person I had the privilege to call my own. As I watched the scene unfold, my head began to feel light and woozy, the world around me spinning in a dizzying dance. I began to sway, my body no longer able to support its own weight. Darkness threatened once again to take over, its tendrils reaching out to pull me into its embrace. As I collapsed, Edith's scream and Emerson's echoing one followed me into the night, their voices fading into the distance as I succumbed to the welcoming arms of unconsciousness.

Chapter 18

When Aurelia collapsed, Emerson cried out her name, a desperate plea torn from his throat as he lurched toward her. His heart pounded with terror, and his vision blurred at the edges. Whatever he intended, his battered body had other ideas. Woozy from pain and blood loss, Emerson crumpled to the ground at his mate's side. The world spun dizzyingly around him as he fought to remain conscious, but the darkness quickly closed in. With a final ragged breath, he surrendered to the waiting oblivion, his body going limp beside Aurelia's still form.

The others in the clearing sprang to action, their movements swift and purposeful. Edith rushed to Arie's side, gently cradling her friend's head in her lap as she checked for signs of life. Her fingers trembled as she brushed a few stray locks of blonde hair from Arie's pale face.

Dominic grabbed Emerson's shoulders, his grip firm yet careful as he assessed the extent of his brother's injuries. Blood seeped from a deep gash on Emerson's forehead, and his breathing was shallow and labored. Edith looked at Dominic, blue eyes wide with fear and concern. She forced herself to take a deep breath, pushing her rising panic to the back of her mind. They needed to stay calm and focused if they were going to help their fallen companions. "She has a pulse."

"So does he. Jace?"

Shedding his physical body, Jace spread his healing light through Arie, letting it suffuse every cell and fiber of her being. As he delved deeper, assessing the extent of the damage, his heart sank with each new discovery. Her injuries were severe, bordering on catastrophic, but he refused to let despair take hold. With unwavering determination and single-minded focus, Jace poured all of his energy into the healing process, heedless of his own wounds and the waning strength that threatened to overtake him. He would not rest until he had done everything in his power to bring Arie back from the brink.

Jace managed to stem the bleeding in her brain, but if he couldn't heal the extensive damage in the rest of her body, she would be lost to them. On top of the grievous injuries, her tainted blood fought against him at each step.

Knowing he had a precious few minutes, he transferred his spirit to Emerson's broken body. The damage was nearly as extensive as Arie's, and Jace worked feverishly to repair what he could with the rapidly dwindling reserves of his own power. He moved as swiftly as possible, but the task was monumental, and his energy was all but spent.

With a shuddering gasp, Jace returned to his own body, swaying on his feet as weakness and blood loss threatened to overtake him. His heart constricted with anguish as he realized the awful truth—he didn't have enough strength or time left to heal them both. With a heavy heart, he tried to find the words to break the terrible news to the others, knowing that a devastating choice would have to be made.

Anya had her palms flat against the ground, her features set in concentration as she listened to the earth. She stood abruptly, straight and tall, with confidence imbued in every word. "We need to take them away from here and give them to the earth."

"The same way Arie healed Emerson before," Reese said. "It's their best chance."

Heartened by the idea, Jace and Dominic wasted no further time arguing. They knew that every second counted if they were to save their fallen friends. With grim determination, they carefully lifted Emerson between them, his head lolling limply against Jace's shoulder. Edith cradled Arie in her arms, the blonde's face ashen and still. Together, they carried Emerson and Arie far enough away that the earth would be untainted from the vicious battle that had felled them.

Anya moved ahead of the somber procession, her keen senses attuned to the living pulse of the land. She scouted for a patch of rich, fertile soil—a place where the regenerative powers of the elements ran strong and deep. Finally, she pointed to a sheltered glade, where the trees parted to reveal a carpet of lush, emerald grass. "There is good."

Setting them gently on the ground, Dominic gripped both of their hands, his fingers interlacing with their cold, lifeless ones. He spoke in a low, steady voice, even knowing they were beyond hearing, the words spilling out of him in a desperate attempt to reach them. "Don't give up. You have to fight. We need you here with us. Please, come back to us."

His voice broke, tears filling his eyes as he pleaded with their still form. Dominic bowed his head and gave them to the waiting embrace of the earth, their last and best hope for survival.

Anya knelt beside them, her hands sinking into the rich, loamy soil. Though Arie had taught her much about the ways of the earth, the power that flowed through Anya now came from a place deep within, guided more by instinct and intuition than training. She closed her eyes, reaching out with her heart and mind, sending her heartfelt plea to Mother Earth. As the others watched, the ground began to quake and shudder, responding to Anya's desperate plea. The tremors grew in intensity, and just as before, the dirt rose up, swirling around the unconscious couple, encasing them in an impenetrable cocoon of earth. The mound solidified, an unbreakable shield against the chaos of life.

They all stood back and stared at what looked like an earthen coffin for several long, agonizing minutes. The group was battered and weary, their bodies crying out for sustenance and needing to heal from the various wounds they'd sustained in the battle. Yet despite their needs, none of them wanted to move, unwilling to leave Arie and Emerson's side in their dire state. The air was heavy with worry and fear, the silence broken only by the occasional ragged breath.

Finally, Reese broke the silence, her voice soft but firm. "You all need to go, feed. I will stay here and keep watch over them."

Dominic's response came swiftly through their mental link, his tone laced with concern and protectiveness. *I won't leave you alone. I can't bear the thought of something happening.*

Reese rubbed Dominic's arm, her touch gentle and reassuring. She understood his reluctance, knowing his decrees stemmed from a deep, abiding love for her and their unborn children. *We'll build a protective barrier around the area, and I promise to stay in it. I'll be safe.*

Unable to come up with a better plan, Dominic finally acquiesced, his shoulders sagging with reluctant acceptance. The others nodded in agreement, and together, they set about creating a shimmering, impenetrable shield around Reese and the earthen mounds.

When she was alone, Reese pulled out her phone with trembling hands. She made a call to push back their travel dates, knowing they would be unable to leave until Arie and Emerson were fully healed. Next, she updated Jade on their situation, her voice catching as she relayed the events of the day.

That done, Reese placed a palm over the mound where the family she never thought she'd have lay on the brink of death. Tears welled in her eyes as she sent a silent prayer to the universe, pleading for their survival. Her other hand came to rest against her stomach, and in that moment, she swore she could feel her unborn daughters pushing out healing energy, their tiny spirits reaching out to their aunt and uncle in a desperate attempt to lend them strength. A flicker of hope bloomed in Reese's chest, and she clung to it like a lifeline in the darkness.

"You will survive this," she said, her tone brooking no argument. "Your family needs you."

STREAMS OF ENERGY DRIFTED THROUGH the soil and spread over the bodies of Emerson and Aurelia like drops of starlight, infusing them with a gentle warmth that seeped into their very bones. Aurelia became aware, and she could tell immediately that she was in a dream state. Besides the soft haziness of the world around her, there was no pain, no aching wounds or throbbing bruises. Or perhaps this was heaven, for when she opened her eyes, Emerson was lying beside her, his handsome face mere inches from her own. His smile lit her soul, chasing away the shadows of worry and fear. "Hello, beautiful."

"Emerson," Aurelia said, placing her palms against his chest, feeling the steady beat of his heart beneath her fingertips. "You're all right."

"Yes. We both are."

"Are we...?"

He shook his head, dark hair falling into his eyes. "No, we're not dead."

"Where are we?" Aurelia gazed at the lush greenery surrounding them, the vibrant colors almost too vivid to be real.

"This is our own private world. Our wounds were grave. The earth is healing us, giving us a place to rest and recover." Emerson's hand found hers, their fingers intertwining.

Aurelia looked down at her smooth skin shown off by the sundress she wore, the fabric light and airy. Emerson sported khaki pants and an unbuttoned white shirt, the material soft and inviting. She pushed the material aside to check his chest for herself, needing to see that he was whole and unharmed.

His hand trapped hers there, his warmth very real even in this made-up place. "This is not how we look in the real world. I woke before you—the earth spoke to me. It will be some time before we are healed."

"How did we get here? The last thing I remember was the fight—you killed the shadowman who killed your parents." Aurelia shuddered at the memory, the image of Emerson's anguished face forever seared into her mind.

"Yes," Emerson said, his hand brushing softly against her cheek, his touch feather-light yet still sending shivers dancing across her skin. "Then you passed out from the pain, and I wasn't far behind. Dominic, Jace, and Edith carried us far from the battle, where Anya asked the earth to help us. She has a unique connection to the earth—like yours, yet different."

"You're sure this isn't heaven?" Aurelia asked with a half-smile.

"It's always heaven, holding you in my arms."

Instead of teasing him, Aurelia gave in to her need and pressed her lips against his, savoring the taste and feel of him. As long as she had Emerson with her, Aurelia knew she could face anything. And if the earth was gifting them this dream world to be together while their physical bodies healed, she would take it and cherish every moment.

It was an incredible feeling to stand and move about free of pain, her body light and unburdened. Here in this dream world, her blood wasn't tainted, her soul wasn't shadowed. Standing, Aurelia offered her hand to Emerson. He accepted, his larger one enveloping hers, his skin warm and slightly calloused. Electricity sparked between them and spread warmth through her insides, a pleasant tingle that only made her feel more alive. Together, they walked along a flowing river, tranquility seeping into her bones with every step.

"This place looks familiar," Aurelia said, gazing about with new eyes, taking in the lush foliage and colorful blooms as Emerson's thumb rubbed soothing circles on the back of her hand. "Does it to you?"

"Not really. It must be something from your memories."

"I think it is," she murmured, brushing her hand along the trunk of a tree, breathing in the scent of passion fruit that hung heavy in the air. "This is Costa Rica. It is the first place Aden brought me to after our parents passed away. This is when I fell in love with traveling, with exploring. He woke that in me, the desire to see the world and all its wonders."

"I wish I could have met him. He sounds like an amazing brother."

"So do I. I miss him every day." Aurelia's heart clenched with a familiar ache, the loss of her brother a wound that would never fully heal.

Following the path of the river, they came upon a waterfall, the strong current casting rainbows at the base, the mist cool and refreshing against their skin. Aurelia waded in, eager to feel the water swirling around her legs. Emerson followed her lead, heedless of the clothes he wore. The water splashed to his waist, plastering his pants to his muscular thighs.

Turning into his arms, Aurelia breathed in his unique scent, unchanged even in their dream world—a mix of sandalwood and something uniquely him. She rested her head against his chest, listening to the strong, steady beat of his heart.

"Emerson, I want to have children with you," she said in a low voice. "After we meet with Reya, Jade, and Kate, if they are able to help me and any children we have are out of danger of Maurice's taint, I want to expand our family. I want to create a life with you filled with love and family."

"That would be the most amazing gift," he murmured against her lips, his breath warm on her skin. "To have a little piece of the two of us to nurture and grow. I want that more than anything."

They came together in a swirl of love, hearts beating as one as their souls knitted back together, two halves of a whole. Everything she had, every piece of her she gave into his keeping, and he took it all with a gentle hand and gave it back tenfold, filling her up until she thought she might burst from the sheer joy of it. Aurelia's heart was so filled with love it burst through her chest, flowing out and around them until it took over their dream world, painting everything in shades of gold and pink.

Aurelia opened her eyes in a daze, meeting those glittering emerald pools she could so easily drown in, so willingly be lost in. Around them, the world softened into a dim light, stars winking in and out of existence like fairies at play, casting a magical glow over everything. "We have forever now, Aurelia. And I intend to spend every moment of eternity worshiping you, loving you with every fiber of my being."

Unable to match his words with her own, Aurelia pressed her lips to his again, pouring all of her thoughts and emotions into the kiss, letting her actions speak for her. Whatever else life brought them, she had this—this perfect moment suspended in time.

Emerson. Her mate, her other half. Her life. Her everything.

Dear Reader,

Thank you so much for reading Aurelia and Emerson's story! It's not quite done yet—next, they'll be meeting with Jade, Talon, and the rest of the Elementals in *Vows at Dusk: Book 7 of The Gifted Series.*

Catch up with all the Elementals we've met so far at Talon and Jade's wedding, plus meet some new ones along the way. We'll be going back to where it all began—Sun Valley, Wisconsin—where magic, love, and a big, nosy family awaits.

There will also be a special bonus novella included called *After Dusk.*

As always, you can keep up-to-date by following me on Facebook, Instagram, or TikTok @AnaBanNovels – or visit my website, www.AnaBanNovels.com

Happy Reading!

Always,

Ana

Other books by Ana Ban

www.anabannovels.com

The Parker Grey Series

Young Adult/Crime Novels recommended for ages 13+

Abstraction; A Parker Grey Novel (Book 1)

Backfire; A Parker Grey Novel (Book 2)

Coercion; A Parker Grey Novel (Book 3)

Deception; A Parker Grey Novel (Book 4)

Dubious Endeavors; A Parker Grey Novella (Book 5)

Exposed; A Parker Grey Novel (Book 6)

Firestarter; A Parker Grey Novel (Book 7)

The Gifted Series

Fantasy Romance Novels recommended for ages 18+

Allure of Home: Book 1 of The Gifted Series

Immaculate: Book 2 of The Gifted Series

Night Shift: Book 3 of The Gifted Series

Stow Away: Book 4 of The Gifted Series

Reservation: Book 5 of The Gifted Series

Shadowed Soul: Book 6 of The Gifted Series

Vows at Dusk: Book 7 of The Gifted Series (with bonus novella, *After Dusk*)

Dark Omens: Book 8 of The Gifted Series

By the Light of the Moon: Book 9 of The Gifted Series

Seeking Redemption: Book 10 of The Gifted Series

Shelter of Smoke: Book 11 of The Gifted Series

Tangled Threads: Book 12 of The Gifted Series

Beyond the Veil: Book 13 of The Gifted Series

Clash at Midnight: Book 14 of The Gifted Series (with bonus novella, *After Midnight*)

Legacy: Book 15 of The Gifted Series

Catching Shadows

Crime/Police Procedural Novel recommended for ages 18+

The Strangers Saga

Murder Mystery Romance Novels recommended for ages 18+

Baton Rouge: Book One

Baton Rouge: Book Two

Baton Rouge: Book Three

Baton Rouge: Book Four

Baton Rouge: Book Five